Scandals for Sale

Publicity man Sid Wallace was fascinated by the scent of success—the smell of good tweeds, plush offices, new money — and his pipeline to prosperity was Harvey Hunsecker, a vindictive Broadway columnist. To get Hunsecker to use items about his clients, Sid would blackmail, cheat or double-cross for him. Even when he was told to smear the man Harvey's sister loved, Sid couldn't make himself quit. He arranged a clever, vicious scandal, and sat back to collect his reward. But payment came from Susan Hunsecker—a startling, savage revenge only a desperate woman in love would attempt!

Piercing the glitter of entertainment headlines, this book about Times Square scandal-mongers is now a powerful, revealing motion picture.

ERNEST LEHMAN is one of Hollywood's best-known scenarists, with many awards for his work on the screenplays of such films as *Somebody Up There Likes Me*, *The King and I*, *Sabrina*, and *Executive Suite*. His novelettes and short stories, which have appeared in leading national magazines, include *The Comedian*, a recent television triumph now planned as a movie.

READ THE BOOK · SEE THE MOVIE

THE PRINCE AND THE SHOWGIRL *by Terence Rattigan*
The exhilarating, indiscreet story of a breezy American showgirl who vamped a prince and changed a whole kingdom's politics in an uproarious royal love affair. Now a lavish Marilyn Monroe-Laurence Olivier film. (#S1409—35¢)

A HATFUL OF RAIN *by Michael Vincent Gazzo*
The unforgettable and widely-acclaimed hit play about a decent young man who is a drug addict, and almost loses his wife when he tries to hide it from her. "There is no resisting the pathos and terror . . ."— Brooks Atkinson, *N. Y. Times* (#S1412—35¢)

LOVE IN THE AFTERNOON (Ariane) *by Claude Anet*
The sophisticated and charming story of an innocent and clever young girl who used an imaginary battery of lovers to confuse—and capture—a seasoned man of the world. (#1404—25¢)

LIZZIE (The Bird's Nest) *by Shirley Jackson*
The brilliant, hilarious, and frightening story of one girl with several separate and warring personalities and her desperate struggle to regain sanity. (#S1400—35¢)

THE BACHELOR PARTY *by Paddy Chayefsky*
The author of *Marty* now writes a powerful story of a bridegroom's carefree stag celebration which explodes into a night of crises for five men—and the women they love. (#S1385—35¢)

TO OUR READERS

SWEET SMELL OF SUCCESS

and other stories

by Ernest Lehman

A SIGNET BOOK

Published by The New American Library

Published as a SIGNET BOOK

FIRST PRINTING, JUNE, 1957

To My Wife

Library of Congress Catalog Card No. 57-11134

*SIGNET BOOKS are published by
The New American Library of World Literature, Inc.
501 Madison Avenue, New York 22, New York*

PRINTED IN THE UNITED STATES OF AMERICA

Contents

The Sweet Smell of Success

I just let her go on talking. I sat there at my desk with the phone propped between my head and shoulder and allowed the insistent monotone of her voice to jab at my brain, while I mopped my forehead with my left hand and tapped a cigarette with my right.

It was one of those dirty, sweltering August afternoons when only two kinds of fools were in their hot city offices: those who had to be, and those who were on the verge of never having to be again, if they played their cards right.

I was tired of being one of those who had to be.

I sat there and listened to her, as I had listened to her for too many years, but now, when the food that had been my lunch began to make itself known to me in sharp little stabs of pain, I knew enough not to let her hit any closer to home. Today of all days, the mirrors had to be kept turned to the wall. The only thing that could go wrong was me, and I was not going to allow that to happen—not today, when all I had been scratching and crawling for was finally drawing within reach.

"Ma . . . . ," I said, "listen . . . Ma . . . please. . . ."

"I know what I'm saying, Sidney. . . ." She went right on talking.

"Ma, will you . . . ?" I tossed the handkerchief on the desk. "Ma, listen to me—"

"Mike was always the smart one. He can see things you and I could never see, not even your poor father could see. If he sees evil—"

7

"Listen here!" I grabbed the phone. "Mike's a kid—
a dumb punk of a kid!"

"Don't shout at me, Sidney. You're not young enough
any more."

"Well, what does *he* know about the world, hidden
away there in college? Who is he to examine every dollar
bill that passes through his hands to make sure it isn't
contaminated by sweat?"

"Not sweat, Sidney. Dirt." Her voice was madden-
ingly calm.

"Look," I said quickly, "my other phone is ringing.
Tell me about it tomorrow."

But she wouldn't let go. "Will you come out and see
me soon?"

"I've told you a hundred times—move to New York.
I'll pay for the apartment. I just don't have the time to
run all the way out to Forest Hills."

"Broadway is your life, not mine. My life is out here
where you can breathe fresh air."

"All right, then. Enjoy it."

"You could call me once in a while."

"For what?" I cried. "To be told by my own family
that I'm not good enough to help them out a bit?"

"What you do, Sidney, you don't do for us. Don't ever
try to fool yourself into thinking *that*."

"Thanks," I said bitterly. "Thank you so much. Now
can I go? I've got work to do."

"You mustn't drive yourself so hard—"

"Yeah, yeah, good-by."

"Try to get more sleep—"

"Okay, okay."

"Eat well."

"Good-by."

"And call me once in a while."

"All *right!*" I hung up quickly.

Outside, the other phone was ringing, and I heard
Gloria answer it.

"Who is it?" I called out.

"I don't know. He won't give his name."

"I'm not in," I said. "I'm not in to anyone."

"It sounds like Steve Dallas," Gloria said.

"Never mind who it sounds like. I'm not in." I wondered whether my voice had betrayed the sudden sinking feeling in my stomach at the mention of his name. It wasn't really a bad sensation, not half as bad as I had thought it would be. But then, I had underestimated myself. All through the years I had held myself back by telling myself there were certain things I'd never be able to go through with.

I picked up the check lying in the junk pile on my desk, and then I took up the letter with which my brother had returned the check and read the letter again for the third time, like a man punching himself in the midriff to prove his own toughness.

Dear Sid:

I doubt if you'll be able to understand it, but I find I can't accept the five hundred. Thanks, anyway, for your generosity. It probably seemed awful to you that I'm working my way through college in a steam laundry, but believe me when I tell you that it isn't bad at all. The nice thing about working in a laundry, Sid, is that it's clean. Also, we work standing up—never on our knees. Get what I mean?

Incidentally, how do you like the way the Dodgers are belting that apple around? If they can keep it up, I have a hunch they'll cop the pennant. Mark my words.

Mike

"I'll mark your words," I muttered, as I tore the letter into little pieces and threw them into the wastebasket. Come to me with the sheepskin in the hand and the worry on the brow and ask me for help, someday, and I'll mark them well. My brother, Michael Wallace, boy Sir Galahad. He had worn the shining armor and pricked me with his sword as far back as I could remember. In the crowded house, no peace. . . .

"Hi, Sid."

"Hello, Mike."

"I saw you at the game yesterday."

"Really? Why didn't you come over and say hello?"

"You were with Hunsecker."

"So?"

"I don't know." He would scuff the carpet as he talked. "I thought maybe you didn't want me around when you were with him."

"Why shouldn't I want you around?" Harshly, as though anger could conceal the truth.

"I don't know," he said to the carpet. "Gee, some game, wasn't it?"

I looked away. "Uh huh."

"How did you like Cramer?"

I didn't answer him. I could feel the blood rising to my cheeks. I knew the silence couldn't last.

"Sid?" he said. "Why did Hunsecker get up and walk out when Cramer had only two more men to face?"

"How do I know?" My voice stuck in my throat.

"Why did he walk out on a no-hit, no-run game with one out in the ninth?" he persisted.

"I guess he wanted to beat the crowds." I walked to the bedroom, but he followed me.

His voice was soft and gentle, like Ma's. "Then why did you get up and leave with him, Sid? You always said—"

"Mind your own business!" I whirled on him.

"You always said you'd give your right arm to see a no-hit, no-run ball game."

"You got a great memory, haven't you?"

"A no-hit, no-run ball game against the Cardinals, and you didn't stay to see the finish," he said smoothly, "just because you're a press agent—and a columnist felt like leaving."

"Okay." I shouted. *"Okay."*

And then he smiled at me, shaking his head slowly . . . the big joke of my brother, Michael Wallace, boy weasel.

I ripped up the check and threw that in the waste-basket, too. He didn't bother me any more. Neither did Ma. They didn't bother me one damned bit.

"Gloria, see if Irving Spahn is back from lunch yet."

"Right."

I picked up the damp handkerchief and wiped my neck. Too much was at stake today, that was the trouble. Somehow I knew that nothing I had ever done for Harvey Hunsecker was as deeply and everlastingly important to him as the favor I had taken it upon myself to do for him now. I had been aware of it from the moment of awakening this morning, feeling the dread in the pit of my stomach and the unwillingness to get out of bed. All morning I had sat at my desk, trying not to think of the afternoon papers that would be out at noon. And when Gloria had finally walked in with them and stacked them up in front of me, it had been ten minutes before I had been able to look at them. Not that I feared the items wouldn't be in. No. Otis Elwell and Leo Bartha were two columnists who could always be counted on to snatch at hunks of raw, red meat if I seasoned them with the proper libel-proof words. What I had really been afraid of was my own reaction to the *fait accompli*, to the evidence in black and white that there was nothing I was not prepared to do, no new level to which I would not descend, in order to sew up Hunsecker's power for me and my clients.

He had come out of the Midwest and, in a few short years, pushed his way close to the pinnacle on which the Winchells and Sullivans perched. While the backs of most columnists had been turned on Broadway and Hollywood and their eyes focused on the more important international scene, Hunsecker had stolen the mantle and proclaimed himself king of show business.

"Hunsecker is not interested in making over the world," he had said to me a few weeks after he arrived from Chicago to join the *Globe*. "Let the others worry about world peace and the United Nations. Hunsecker is interested in Hunsecker." Then he had fixed his gimlet eyes on me and added shrewdly, "If you are a bright boy, Sidney—and I think you are—you will be interested in Hunsecker, too."

Privately, I had scoffed. But that was five years ago. Nobody scoffed now. The word was "obeisance." The entertainment world genuflected to his skyrocketing circulation and expanding influence with all the reverence it could muster. And he had achieved it all merely by adding new and scabrous meanings to the word "rumor."

"Irving Spahn on one," Gloria called out.

I picked up the phone. "Irv, baby? Sidney."

"What is it?"

"You sound funny, Irv."

"I wonder why," he said stiffly. "You can't think of any reason why, can you, Sidney? I guess you haven't seen the papers yet, is that it?"

"I never read them, baby, unless I figure on having something in, and today is not one of those days."

"You haven't got the papers there?"

"No," I said.

There was a moment of silence. "All right, then," he said. "Let me read something to you." I heard him rustling the papers. "Let me read you the lead item of a cockroach by the name of Otis Elwell. Are you listening, Sidney?"

"Go ahead."

He read, " 'That loud noise you are about to hear is the career of a certain crooner going up in smoke—marijuana smoke—and it's not going to help business at that East Side spot where he is currently flying high when they also discover he's the life of the party—Communist, that is.' "

I said, "Yeah? So—?"

"Wait a minute," he said savagely, "don't go away. Let me read you this, from the column of the little Napoleon, my *friend* Leo Bartha, for whom I've done favors. Just listen."

"I'm listening, baby."

"My friend Leo Bartha writes, 'The peculiar smoking habits of a highly touted newcomer to the Stem are giving a bad stench to the elegant *boîte* where he sings. Naughty, naughty, fellah. That's no way for a card-holding Party member to act.' "

I examined my fingernails. I needed a manicure. "Who do they mean?"

"Who do they mean?" His voice shook suddenly. "I don't know who they mean. Do *you* know who they mean, Sidney? I don't know who they mean, and maybe *they* don't know who they mean either, but everybody else thinks they mean Steve Dallas. *That's* who they mean!"

"Steve Dallas? You're out of your mind!" I gave it a good reading. "Dallas a Commie? Dallas with reefers? That boy? Don't be silly, Irv."

"Listen to me, Sidney." He fought to get his voice

under control. "Do you think I'm a fool? I know it isn't true. I know that boy better than I know myself. He's a fine kid. But people read the columns, and they believe what they read. That's all that matters. And it just so happens that when you read those items the first name that pops into your mind is Steve Dallas. I don't know why. *It just so happens* that's the way they're worded."

It just so happens. . . .

"Where do you suppose Elwell and Bartha picked up that kind of smear stuff, Irv?"

"They never reveal a source. Remember, Sidney?"

I waited.

"Sidney?"

"Yeah, Irv?"

"You have any idea what this might be all about?"

"Well . . . no . . . ," I answered slowly. "Not exactly . . . but . . ."

"But what?"

"Well, I was just thinking. You know how jealous Elwell and Bartha are of Hunsecker's syndication, and how much they resent the fact that he's managed to do in a few years what they've been trying to do for a lifetime. . . ."

"Go on, I'm listening."

"I was just thinking—they're like malicious kids. Maybe they put the blast on Dallas because he's been seen around town lately with Susan Hunsecker. Maybe they would louse up your boy just to get back at Hunsecker through his kid sister."

"You talk very funny, Sidney."

"Huh?"

"I was always under the impression that Hunsecker tells you everything, even what he dreams when he goes to sleep. You talk as though you don't know Hunsecker is not at all happy about this romance. You talk as though you don't know what's going on."

"That has nothing to do with it," I said quickly. "What you and I know is one thing. What other people know is another thing. I'm telling you Elwell and Bartha might very well think—"

"Sidney—"

"What?"

"I'd hate to tell you what *I* think about all this." His voice started going again. "I'm afraid to tell you what's in my mind—"

"Now, baby, don't let your imagination start running away with you. Relax."

"All right, Sidney, I'll relax," he said brokenly. "I'll forget that Van Cleve called me five minutes after the papers hit the stands. I'll forget that he wants to see me and the boy this afternoon. 'What about?' I asked. 'Never mind what about,' he said, 'just be there.' He doesn't have to tell me what about. I know. I can tell by his voice. In ten minutes, I'm going over there to be told that Dallas is through at the Elysian Room. And that's only the beginning. The word is out already. He'll be through all over town—"

"Now, baby—"

"Do you know what that means, Sidney?" he cried. "I got two kids and Grace is not well enough to work. I don't have a Harvey Hunsecker in my pocket. I don't have anything in my pocket. All I got in the world is a piece of this boy Dallas, and it could be a gold mine someday, because he's got everything—*everything*—and now it's all going out the window!"

"Listen, Irv—"

"And for why, Sidney? Why?"

"Baby, listen to me—"

"What did I do? What did *he* do to deserve this?"

"Wait a minute, Irv. Use your common sense. It's not as bad as all that. Maybe he'll lose a booking or two, but that's all. A couple of blind items in a couple of second-rate columns can't ruin a talent like that. Nobody will remember it a week from now. And the minute those jealous, spiteful slobs see that your boy isn't interested in Hunsecker's sister any more, they'll lay off him and look for new targets. They'll—"

"What was that you said, Sidney?" He spoke slowly, carefully.

"I said it would take more than a couple of second-rate items to ruin a talent like that."

"No, Sidney, no. Something else you said. That wasn't all you said."

I took a deep breath. I had tried—really tried. "And I

said that nothing bad will happen to Dallas providing he forgets about Susan Hunsecker." I swallowed. "Nothing permanent, Irv."

There was a moment of terrible silence, the worst silence I had ever heard. "Sidney," he groaned. "My God—Sidney. . . . You and me—" He choked up. "We were kids together. We played on the same basketball team—the same school—we went out on double dates together. Sidney, we starved together. Didn't you remember? This is me—Irv Spahn—you did this to. Don't you remember all the things—?" He started slobbering.

"Irv!" I shouted. "Listen to me!"

"All right," he wailed, "I'm listening! I'm listening! Go ahead. What can I do now but listen?"

I waited, while he blew his nose and tried to pull what was left of himself together.

"Now look, baby," I said in a soothing voice, "use your common sense. You're his agent. You're his best friend. Speak to the boy. He'll listen to you. Tell him to give up the girl and everything will be all right. Nothing else will happen if he gives up the girl. Nothing at all. Now will you please be sensible and talk to the boy?"

The words came back to me dry and hollow, drained of everything there had ever been between us. "All right," he said stiffly. "I'll—I'll speak to him. I'll see what I can do."

"You're my friend, baby, and I have a lot of respect for the boy, and I don't like to see you get into any kind of trouble. You know that, Irv, don't you?"

He made a funny little sound in his throat.

"Irv? Don't you?"

The phone went dead.

As I mopped my forehead, I felt the pains stabbing at my insides again.

"Gloria," I called quickly, "bring your pad in."

She came in silently and stood before the desk gazing at me.

"What's the matter, Mr. Wallace?"

I scowled. "What do you mean, 'What's the matter?' "

"You don't look well. You look kind of—kind of—funny."

"How do you expect me to look in this heat?" I

snapped. "Or maybe you didn't know it was hot today. I tell you everything else, maybe I even have to tell you it's hot today!"

"I'm sorry." She gave me the wounded look. "I only meant—"

"Never mind what you meant. If I want to know how I look, I can go to the mirror. Now, I want this on the blue memo paper. I want it to go to Leo Bartha and Otis Elwell right away, by messenger." I wiped my neck dry as I dictated. "Sweetheart: Just want you to know . . . that I did give it to you exclusive. . . . (Put 'did' in caps.) Don't ask me how he got it, too. ('He' in caps.)"

" 'Sweetheart:' " Gloria read back. " 'Just want you to know that I DID give it to you exclusive. Don't ask me how HE got it, too.' "

She waited, with pencil poised.

"That's all," I said.

"But—what do I send to Elwell?"

"The same thing. It goes to both of them."

She looked at me strangely. "To both of them?"

"To both of them," I said, holding her gaze.

She just stood there, staring at me.

"Is there any question, Gloria?" I asked harshly. "Is there something you'd like to say, perhaps?"

She turned away.

"Because if there is," I called after her, "I don't want to hear it."

She had been a great help to me in the early days, when a little thing like being able to ask your secretary to wait a few weeks for her salary often meant the difference between staying in business and folding. But I had a feeling now that we had worked together too long. She was part of the old order. I'd be needing someone now whose big brown eyes carried no reflections, someone who would not expect me to be a person I could no longer afford to be.

I glanced at my watch. Five after four. The column proof would be ready. I buttoned my collar, pulled my tie into a knot, and took my jacket from the hanger.

"I'll be at Hunsecker's office," I said to Gloria as I went past her desk.

"Will you be back?"

"Why?"

"Well, it's so hot. I thought—I thought maybe I could leave early."

"Not today."

"Most of the girls in the other offices—"

"I'll be back," I said, "but if anyone calls, I'm gone for the day. Got it?"

"Yes," she said quietly.

I walked down the hall to the elevator and pressed the "Down" button.

Of course I looked bad.

I shrugged inwardly.

Who wouldn't, in this heat?

II

The sky was growing dark, and thunder rumbled closer. I quickened my steps as I walked west to the *Globe* building. The sidewalks were steaming and the air was heavy with exhaust fumes, but still it was good to be outside, away from the fetid odors of old newspapers and dirty walls and Gloria's cheap toilet water. When I got my new office, it would have thick carpeting and rich, bleached-oak furniture, and the air would be scented with the sweet smell of success.

As I rode up in the elevator to the twenty-second floor, I could feel the cold knot of tension hardening inside of me the way it always did when I was about to see an advance proof of Hunsecker's column. Always there was that hope that he had come through for me; always, the knowledge that even if he hadn't, I'd go on catering to him just the same. But soon all that would be different. The uncertainty would be a thing of the past. Perhaps I wouldn't even be needing Mary any more as my ticket of admission to the preview.

She was on the phone when I walked in, and her face lighted up as she saw me.

I pointed to the phone. "Him?"

She shook her head, whispering, "He's still asleep."

I sauntered idly about the office, staring at the photographs on the wall of Hunsecker playing golf with the mighties of the show world. I deliberately avoided the proof lying there on the desk.

Finally, Mary hung up and called, "Hello, sweetie."

I turned and blew her a kiss. "Just passing by."

"Oh, come." She got up, eyes searching mine anxiously. "No real one?"

I took her in my arms, feeling the dampness of my shirt. "How are you, honey?"

"A little angry," she murmured. Her lips tasted salty, and I drew away and walked to the window. "Why didn't you call, Sidney?" Her voice trailed me. "I waited home all night. You said you would. What happened?"

I wiped my mouth on my sleeve. "I had to work late," I said to the window. "You know how it is, Mary."

But she didn't, really. Not yet, she didn't.

"But, Sidney, couldn't you at least have called to say—?"

I turned from the window. "Baby!" I spread out my hands. "In this heat—arguments?"

She came to me quickly, her face set in a smile of nervous appeasement, her hands fumbling with my tie. "I'm not arguing, dear. I just want you to know how much I miss you when I don't hear from you, that's all. I know it's foolish of me to let you know, but that's the way I am, Sidney." She turned away suddenly. "Foolish."

I glanced at my wrist watch. "Well . . ."

"Don't you want to see the column?"

I shrugged. "Okay."

I walked slowly to the desk, my whole body taking part in the elaborate ritual of disinterest, and I picked up the proof.

It never did me any good to tell myself that this was just a piece of paper with some ink marks on it, that these words would soon be as forgotten as yesterday's headlines. Because I knew how much weight these words carried wherever they were read. I knew how savagely people of otherwise normal good sense fought with each other to carve a slice of this young and growing empire for themselves.

But today I didn't have to bother to tell myself anything at all. Today, as my eyes flickered down the column looking for the familiar symbols that were my clients' names, and found none of them, I felt hardly any of the bitterness I usually felt at being shut out. The bitterness was tinged with optimism now. It was colored with the future. I was being chastised, and I knew it, but I didn't mind. I was being told, in the only way Hunsecker knew that I could be convinced, that this was to be my lot as long as I failed to please him.

I did not intend to fail to please him.

"What time did he go to bed this morning?" I asked, without looking up from the column.

"Ten-thirty," Mary said. "You should have heard him, Sidney. He—"

"Then he didn't see the afternoon papers, did he?"

"No. He went right to bed. I called his apartment at eleven, and Nikko said he was fast asleep."

"I see."

"You should have heard him this morning, Sidney. The way he carries on about Susan and that boy. With so many important things on his mind, that's all he talked about for a half hour. My arm went numb holding the phone. Today he asked me if I thought it would be wise to send her abroad for a year. She doesn't want to go back to college, you know. And, frankly, I don't blame her. I think it's nice to be in love when you're young. I think when two people are in love they should get married, don't you, Sidney?"

"Uh huh," I said to the proof.

"I don't know what the chief has against Steve. What if he *doesn't* have any money? What if he *is* young and struggling? That shouldn't make any difference. I know it wouldn't make any difference to me. I wouldn't care really. Sidney—"

"This item here," I said, looking up. "Who is Herbie Temple's press agent?"

"Herbie Temple? No one, as far as I know. Why?"

I waved the column. "Then how come this plug? How did it get in?"

She looked vague.

I read it to her. " 'If there's a more hilarious funnyman

in the world than Herbie Temple at the Viking, you'll have to pardon us for not catching the name. We're too busy screaming.' "

"Oh, him. The chief heard him the other day and was raving about him to me, so I said, 'Why don't you say something in the column? It might be a nice thing to do.' And he did. That's all."

I grunted. "Since when does he bother to see the performers he praises?"

"Don't get fresh," she pouted. Then she smiled quickly. "After all, he *is* my boss, and I do take my life in my hands letting you come up here to see the column in advance." The smile faded. "And it looks as though I'm going to need a boss, and a job, forever."

I tossed the proof back on the desk. "Gotta run."

"So soon?"

"Busy, busy."

"Sidney . . ." Her voice clung to me.

"Come on. Walk me to the elevator."

"My phone might ring."

"He's asleep."

She took my arm as we walked. "Sidney, is anything— wrong?"

"Wrong? What do you mean, 'wrong'?"

She averted her gaze. "You know—with us?"

I pressed the button. "Of course not, honey."

"You seem to be changing."

"I'm getting older," I laughed.

"So am I," she said, not laughing.

Through the window at the end of the hall, I saw a sudden flash of lightning. I was going to get caught in the rain if I didn't hurry.

Outside, big drops had started spattering down. I jumped into a cab and headed back to the office.

"Wait a minute," I said to the driver; "do you mind going by way of Fifty-fourth Street?"

"It's your money, not mine." He shrugged. "I'll even go by way of Canarsie."

The skies had opened up a deluge now, and people were scurrying for shelter.

"Whaddaya think of them Dodgers?" the cabbie asked.

"You don't happen to have a paper up front, do you?" I asked.

"Yeah, sure. My fares always leave 'em. Here." He handed me one.

"Thanks." I took it and turned to the amusement page.

"It don't have the late scores, though. But I can tell you—the Yankees and Giants lose. The Brooks, they win. Nine in a row today. Seven to one they beat the Pirates."

The Viking stage show went on at 6:38.

I handed the paper back through the window. "Thanks."

"Ya know, the way they're going, they got a damn good chance of grabbing off another pennant. Whaddaya think of that?"

"What's that?"

"The Bums," he said. "The way they're going they're liable to—"

"I'm not interested in baseball," I said quickly.

"I was only saying—"

"Look, I'm not interested," I said. "Do you mind?"

"Okay, mister." He turned around to stare at me for a moment. "Okay."

"Would you please slow down as you pass the Elysian Room?"

"Anything you say."

People were huddled glumly beneath the Elysian canopy, waiting hopefully for a cab. To the right of the entrance stood the billboard frame in which, for the past four weeks, the softly compelling features of Steve Dallas had been displayed, with the strip across one corner stating simply: "Nightly . . . At Dinner . . . and Supper." Everything about the Elysian Room, even its billboard, was in the best of taste. That was what Emil Van Cleve was selling, chiefly—the illusion that, by coming here, one automatically acquired that good taste, too. It was the kind of illusion that perished easily, and it had to be guarded with care.

The billboard was empty now. Steve Dallas had been removed—blown away by the bad breath of scandal.

"Okay," I said to the cabbie. "Full speed ahead." I was glad that he didn't turn around to look at me. I must have looked pretty silly sitting there in the back of a cab, crawling through a crashing thunderstorm on a hot summer afternoon, with a smile on my sweating face.

The smile was gone by the time I was moving down the hall to my office. I walked in fast, as though needing momentum to carry myself across the unwanted threshold, and then it was too late to turn around. She saw me right away.

"Susan, honey . . ." My mouth went dry. She got up from the sofa. "How long have you been waiting?" I took her hand. It was cold.

"Not long. I want to talk to you." Her voice was even colder.

"Sure. I'll be right with you. A couple of minutes. Just you sit here." I eased her back on the sofa and turned to Gloria. Her face was white. "Come inside, please," I said tonelessly.

She followed me in, and I closed the door and turned on her.

"Didn't I tell you I was gone for the day?" I cried in a fierce whisper.

"I told her," Gloria pleaded, "but she wouldn't believe me. She insisted on waiting."

"You could have called me. You knew where I was."

"But—but I didn't think—"

"You didn't think. You never think. That's the trouble with you. Well, let me tell you something. You better start thinking fast—about what's going to become of you" —I looked away—"because I can't go on like this much longer."

I heard her suck in her breath.

"And don't start crying," I said, "because that won't help."

She stood there speechless.

"That's all I need around here today—tears." I looked back at her. Her lips were trembling. "Well, go on, it's too late now. Tell her to come in."

"Yes, Mr. Wallace." She hurried out of the room.

I hung up my jacket and loosened my tie, as though that would make things any easier.

"Susan, honey, I'm all yours." She came in briskly, looking cool in a black dress and a sun tan that went well with her golden hair. "Lucky for you I changed my mind and decided to come back to the office. Sit down and talk to me. What have you been doing? Tell me about everything."

"Oh, Sidney"—she walked up to me and looked me right in the eyes—"why did you do it? How could you have been so stupid?"

I looked right back at her. The loveliness was still fresh, but a trace of hardness had crept into her face. A summer in New York—with Harvey . . . "What are you talking about?"

"Please," she said impatiently, "please. Don't you think I know? Don't you think Steve knows? I'm past anger now. I'm amazed that you think you can get away with it, that you think it would make any difference to us."

I lighted a cigarette. "You know Harvey doesn't like you to come up here," I said. "You know how angry he gets."

"Stop it, Sidney."

"Stop what?"

"Stop trying to be a pale imitation of my brother. You weren't born to it. You haven't got the makings. That's what I came here for—to warn you to stop trying to be another Harvey Hunsecker."

"Now, is that a nice way to talk?"

"One thing I'll say for you: You have the guts to do your own dirty work. Or is it that you're not big enough yet to have your own hatchet men? Maybe you haven't been at it long enough, but you'll get there."

"Sit down, Susan," I said, feeling the pounding of my heart. "You make me nervous, pacing up and down like a wild animal."

"I'll sit down when I want to."

"You're acting very childish," I said. "You're talking very much like a little child who is angry because she can't have everything her own way."

She turned on me. "This *is* everything!" she cried hotly. "It's my whole life! Steve and I love each other, and we're going to get married. Yes, married!" She said it right to my white, protesting face. "And I'm telling you to lay off, Sidney, because it won't do any good. You can't stop us. Nothing can stop us. We're getting married even if it means that Steve won't be able to earn one single dollar in show business. He'll give up his career. He'll do something else. Anything. We love each other in a way that you and Harvey could never understand, so don't try to stop us, Sidney. I'm warning you! It means too much to me!"

She twisted away and hid her face, and for a moment she was a frightened child, a little girl making great big speeches. I seized that moment to get up and walk over to her and put my arm around her shoulder. "Look, honey," I said softly, "listen to me."

She shuddered convulsively and drew away. "Don't touch me!"

"All right, Susan," I shrugged. "All right."

I went to the window and stared out at the retreating storm. It was somewhere over Long Island now, and the last drops of rain were petering out. It should have felt cooler in the office, but it didn't. It was hotter and more oppressive than ever. I sat down at the desk and tried her again.

"There's something you've got to understand about Harvey," I said in a quiet voice.

She turned to me. "Do tell me," she broke out defiantly. "I didn't grow up in the same house with him. I never heard what people used to say about him, and I haven't seen him in action here in New York all summer. So do tell me, Sidney. I'm only his sister."

I brushed it aside, shaking my head. "The worst thing you can ever do to Harvey is show him that he's wrong. If you want to win him over, you have to give him an out, you have to let him save face." I paused. "Now, I honestly think he realizes that he has been a little foolish about all this—"

"Please." She shook her head. "Please."

"—and I'm certain that if you just give him time—time and the chance for a graceful retreat—"

"How, Sidney?" She threw me a quizzical glance. "Just how do you propose that I do this?"

"Well . . ." I groped and came up with it. "Perhaps if you went away for a while . . ."

"Yes, go on," she prodded me.

"A trip to Europe. You've never been there, have you? Maybe even a trip around the world—"

"Wonderful!" She threw up her hands in bitter laughter. "Absolutely and positively priceless. The two of you ought to go into vaudeville together."

"Now, listen to me—" Enough was enough.

"No, you listen to *me*, Sidney." She put her hands on the desk; her eyes were blazing. "You're still making the big mistake of underestimating me. I can see that you don't know me any better than you know Harvey."

I had to laugh in her face. That was a hot one. *I* didn't know Harvey. That was even hotter than the weather. "Suppose *you* tell *me*, then."

"Didn't you see his face that very first night I met Steve—that night at the Panamanian, when Steve came over to the table and asked if he might dance with me?"

If only she had said no. . . .

"Can't you even remember how he acted, Sidney, the day I ran into you on Fifth Avenue, when I asked you to take me to lunch, and he found out about it later from someone else?"

Yes. He had gone into a frenzy, over nothing at all. . . .

"I still don't see what all this—"

"It's too bad you weren't there the night—oh God, when I think of it now! We were living in Chicago then. I was fifteen years old and this boy took me home from a party, and Harvey opened the door and caught us kissing in the hall outside. Freddie Meadley was the boy's name. I never forgot it. And I'll never forget the look on Harvey's face, and the way he screamed and tore into that poor boy and pounded his head on the stone floor as though he wanted to kill him. It was frightful, Sidney. He would have killed the boy without even knowing what he was doing if the elevator man hadn't come up to see what the noise was about. And Harvey didn't say a word to me. He just slapped my face and walked back into the apartment and didn't speak to me for weeks."

"Susan, look—" I squirmed in my chair.

"Sidney"—her face came closer—"what makes you think Harvey wants me to marry *anyone—ever*?"

"Don't talk nonsense."

"What makes you think he'll ever come to realize that I'm not that fifteen-year-old girl any longer, and that he can't hoard me like a miser? How long am I supposed to remain the shining image, the untouched maiden? Look at me, Sidney."

But I couldn't.

"Why has he always sent me away to girls' schools— nunneries in disguise? Why did he insist I go to a college for women when I wanted to go to a coed place?" She jabbed at me. "When I came to New York this summer, why wouldn't he let me stay at a hotel? Why did he ruin the perfectly beautiful study in his own apartment and turn it into a bedroom so that I'd be living under his watchful eye?"

I didn't answer her.

"Why, Sidney?" Her voice grew more insistent. "Tell me—*why?*"

I was seeing Hunsecker's contorted face and hearing the sickening thud of a head pounded against stone and the savage screams of a man possessed.

"What do you mean, why?" I looked up at her in desperate anger. "He's always thinking of what's best for you, that's why. Because he loves you!"

"Love!" She tore the word apart harshly. "Exactly what he always said. I've got advice for you, Sidney. I've got advice for the world. Don't be a late baby if you can help it. Don't get born so late that your parents are never anything but elusive memories and well-kept graves. A brother makes a rotten father and mother, especially if he also happens to be Harvey Hunsecker. That's why I'm pulling clear of him for good. Let him drive Steve out of show business. Let him hound me to the ends of the earth and deprive me of the dubious benefits of being a sister to the famous. I'm getting married, Sidney. To-morrow!"

I jumped up from the chair. "Tomorrow!"

"Yes." She laughed, a little hysterically. "Surprised, aren't you? I wasn't going to tell you." She struggled to open her handbag. "I haven't told Harvey and I don't intend to."

"You'll break his heart."

"I'm telling you, Sidney, because I can see that you don't understand people very well. You still might do something foolish if you believe there's a chance to frighten us off. I want you to know it won't do any good."

She handed me a paper. "I just want you to know for sure."

I took it. It was a marriage license. It would be valid tomorrow. I stared at it, at the awful finality of the words printed there.

"Susan, look—" My voice was hoarse.

"Oh, please," she cried eagerly, "say 'Congratulations.' Wish me luck. Please, I want to hear someone say they're happy to hear about it. Just once, please."

"Why do you want to ruin the boy's life? Harvey will never rest! You know what will happen to Dallas before Harvey's through. Do you think the boy will be able to love you under those conditions?" I went to her quickly and took her arm. "Don't do it, honey. Wait. Give me time. I'll talk to Harvey. Just give me time. Don't run away with the boy. Harvey will never forgive you."

"Never forgive *me?* Or never forgive *you?* Is that what you're worried about?"

"Susan, you've got to promise me—"

"Sidney." She cut me short.

I searched her eyes. They were cold.

"Stop playing with hatchets," she said. "You weren't meant for it. You'll only cut yourself."

She drew away from me and opened the door.

I went after her, past Gloria's desk. "You don't know what you're doing—!"

"For the first time in my life, I really do," she called back, "and I'll never forgive you, Sidney, for not wishing me luck. It's still possible I'll need all I can get."

I stood there watching her walk down the hall, a slip of a girl playing a grown-up game. I could have followed her, but I knew it wouldn't have done any good—not when they were as young as she was. That was the trouble with them before they grew up and learned about the world they lived in—their brains were in their hearts.

I turned to Gloria. "Get me Irving Spahn."

"Is anything the—?"

"Quickly." I went inside and sank down at my desk. My hands were shaking. I was thinking about what would happen if Steve Dallas had no common sense either, and somehow I knew he hadn't. He was too young. But I had to go through the motions.

I sat there waiting, and finally Gloria came in.

"Mr. Spahn doesn't want to speak to you," she said, looking at me queerly. "He said it was no use. He said he tried, but it was no use, and he has nothing to say."

"All right," I said dully.

"Mary called while you were—in conference."

I looked up.

"She said Mr. Hunsecker is awake. He's having his breakfast at Babe Scanlon's in an hour."

I glanced at my watch.

"He wants you to meet him there."

"All right," I said, staring blankly out of the window. "I'll be there."

The important thing was to act as though everything were all right, as though everything were going off right on schedule. It wasn't over yet. There were further levels to climb down to. . . .

I took my coat off the hanger.

"Mr. Wallace?"

"What is it?"

"Can I go home now?"

"No," I said. "I'll call in." I turned. "And Gloria, when I phone you, don't say anything, just listen. You got that straight? Just listen."

"Yes, Mr. Wallace."

There was no reason to underestimate oneself, no reason to give up. There wasn't even any reason not to stop off at the Viking on the way.

III

The geezer at the stage-door entrance held his arm out in front of me. "Just a second. You can't go in there."

"That's right, Pop," I said, "and *you* can't buy a Cadillac convertible with *this*."

He took the ten and shrugged.

Herbie Temple was sitting at the mirror when I walked into the dressing room, covering the scars of too many years of obscurity with a thick layer of pancake. Al Evans was pacing back and forth behind him, straining his worried voice through an unlighted cigar.

I pointed a finger at Evans. "Hiya, tootsie."

He looked up with a grunt of displeasure. "I didn't know you and Herbie knew each other," he muttered.

"We don't," I grinned. "How do you do, Mr. Temple?"

The comedian got to his feet quickly and, because there was no telling who I was, he hung a smile on his lean, aging face.

"My name is Sidney Wallace."

"Delighted."

Evans looked at the tip of his cigar. "Mr. Wallace is a press agent."

The smile was still there, but it had suddenly congealed. I sat down on the studio couch.

Al Evans said, "Look, pappy, Herbie and me here were having a little talk, a sort of private business talk, you might call it."

"Earning your ten per cent, Al?" I looked right past his frown to Temple, who was back in front of the mirror with the pancake sponge. "I caught your act the other night, Mr. Temple."

"Did you, now?" he said flatly. "On which bounce?"

"Ha ha—and I just had to drop by to tell you how positively great I thought you were. Great."

Temple just stared at himself in the mirror. Then he said, "What time is it, Al?"

"You got fifteen minutes, Herbie."

"That's all?" He turned to me. "Then I'm sure Mr.— what did you say your name was?"

"Crosby," I said. "Bing Crosby."

"I'm sure Mr. Frannis-on-the-portisan will excuse us now, Al."

Evans looked at me. "If you don't mind, Wallace—"

I got up. "Certainly," I said. "But can I ask just one teeny-weeny question?"

"Now, please—"

"How come you're allowing a sock act like Herbie Temple to tiptoe through town without a publicity campaign?"

Al Evans gave me the wise, all-knowing smile and shook his head slowly. "Unh-uh, Wallace. We don't want any today. No fish today."

"But, baby," I spread out my hands, "I'm not selling. I'm just curious, that's all."

"Answer the man, Al," Temple said to the mirror. "The man says before he goes he just wants to ask one question, so answer the man before he thinks of another."

Evans had my arm and was easing me toward the door. "Herbie doesn't believe in press agents," he said. "Does that answer it for you?"

"You got one word too many in there, Al," said Temple. "Herbie doesn't believe press agents. Unquote."

I turned. "I know exactly how you feel, Mr. Temple. They all claim they're going to do so much for you, and they never do. You might say there's a broken promise for every light on Broadway—"

"*You* might. *I* never would."

"—and about the only thing I can say for myself is that when *I* tell a prospective client how I'm going to get Hunsecker to take care of him, it's not just talk."

It was wonderful, the way Evans' hand relaxed its pressure on my arm and Temple's pancake sponge paused in midair at precisely the same word—the magic word, Hunsecker.

Without waiting, I stepped to the telephone quickly, saying, "I know you don't believe me."

"Here. Wait a minute," Evans cried.

"Let him alone, Al." Temple put down the sponge and turned to watch me.

I dialed my office and waited. Gloria answered on the third ring.

I said, "Mr. Hunsecker, please."

"What? Who is this?"

"Mr. Wallace. Sidney Wallace. I want to talk to Mr. Hunsecker. It's important." I stopped listening to her confusion and put my hand over the mouthpiece.

"Look," Evans said, moving toward me, "we haven't hired you. We didn't talk any deal here—"

"Relax, baby," I said. "I told you—I'm not selling anything. Not a thing."

Gloria had fallen silent.

"Hello, Harvey? Sidney. How're you, sweetheart? Good —good . . . attaboy. Listen, Harvey, are you through with the column yet? . . . Oh, you are? . . . Well, look, it isn't too late to add something, is it? . . . I know, I know, but you can always throw something out, can't you?

You've done it for me before. . . . Of course it's important.
Would I ask you if it wasn't? . . . All right then. You
know Herbie Temple? . . . What do you mean, what
about him? He's at the Viking, and he's great, *that's* what
about him, and I want you to say something about him in
tomorrow's column. . . ."

I saw Temple and Evans exchange quick glances.

"Harvey. . . . Listen to me, Harvey. . . . I know, but
. . . I know, but that's beside the point. I want you to do it
for *me*. . . . No, next week will be too late. Tomorrow.
. . . Yes . . . Okay. Got a pencil there? . . . Just say, uh, let's
see. . . . 'If there's a more hilarious funnyman in the world
than Herbie Temple . . . at the Viking . . . uh . . . you'll
have to pardon us for not catching the name . . . uh . . .
we're too busy laughing.' No, make that 'screaming.' . . . I
sure will, sweetheart . . . Right, baby . . . Oh, say, Harvey,
where you having dinner? . . . In twenty minutes? I think
I could. . . . Why, sure, I'd love to. . . . Fine. Swell. Babe
Scanlon's in twenty minutes."

I hung up and looked from one blank, staring face to
the other.

"See what I mean?" I said to Herbie Temple. And for
one brief, ridiculous instant I hoped that he wouldn't.
I hoped that somehow he'd show me that Harvey Hunsecker meant nothing to me. But it was an instant that
was gone almost before it came.

Temple swung back to the mirror, saying, "Speak to
him, Al."

I moved to the door. "We'll have you in pictures in
no time, Mr. Temple," I said. "Don't worry about a
thing."

"Al makes the deals. Speak to Al," he said.

"I got a dinner date, didn't you hear?" I said. "Plenty
of time tomorrow. You know where my office is, Al."

"Yeah," the agent said coldly, looking at me with hard,
suspicious eyes, "why don't we wait until tomorrow?"

I gave the man at the stage door a big good-by on the
way out. He didn't know it, but he was a bargain.

The dinner mobs were lined up twelve deep at Babe
Scanlon's.

Herman gave me an unseeing glance.

"I'm dining with Mr. Hunsecker," I said. "He expects me."

The waters parted. "Oh, right this way, please, Mr. Wallace."

He didn't really have to lead me. I knew which table Hunsecker was at. There were always at least three waiters hovering over him, like buzzards circling a carcass. Any day I expected to find one of them waving a palm frond over the table.

I slid into a chair. "Hello, Harvey."

He looked up and grunted as he continued to shovel the food into his mouth.

I took up the bill of fare.

He pointed his fork at one of the waiters. "Bring him the same," he commanded, "but tell them out there to put a little more garlic in the sauce."

"I don't think I feel like that tonight," I said.

He cast his eyes on me for a moment, and then he turned back to the waiter. "And see that the onions are chopped fine. You want iced coffee with that?"

I tossed the menu down. "All right," I said. "Iced coffee."

"Now tell the other two Marx brothers to get lost." The waiters shuffled away obediently.

"All right. Come on." He snapped his fingers. "Get it over with. Take your bow before the food comes."

I looked up at him. "You saw the items?"

"Of course I saw them. I always read the opposition. It's like reading my wastebasket, or last week's column."

"Steve Dallas is through at the Elysian Room," I announced quietly.

He forced a dill pickle into his mouth. "Well? Go on. Go on."

"What do you mean, go on? He's out, and the freeze is setting in on him."

"I'm still listening," Harvey said.

"What do you want me to tell you?"

"I want to hear that it's all over, that the towel is in the ring. I'm not interested in the state of his employment. I don't like words like 'freeze.' They're too vague. They don't cool me off a bit. Talk plainer, Sidney."

I clutched at my napkin. I didn't answer. There was nothing else to say.

"Talk louder, Sidney."

Tell him. Go on. Maybe he'll give up and free you. Tell him now, before it's too late. If he doesn't give up now . . .

"Harvey look—" My lips were trembling. "I—saw Susan today."

He sucked in his breath. "What? Where?"

"In my office."

His hand shot out across the table and grabbed my lapel. "I told you I didn't want her up there!" he snarled.

"I didn't ask her to come, Harvey, I—"

"Who was she with?"

"She was alone."

He pulled me closer. "Alone? Just you and she?" A man at the next table turned, startled at his tone.

"I have a secretary, Harvey." My voice was hoarse. "Her name is Gloria. Remember?"

He threw my lapel back at me. It was damp with perspiration.

"Well, come on, what for?" he snapped. "What was she there for?"

"To talk to me." I straightened my tie.

"Talk? What about?" he cried. "What would you two have to talk about? Answer me, Sidney! What did she tell you?"

I stared at him for a moment. He'll understand. He'll know when to give up. "It's no use, Harvey. She's leaving you. She says she's marrying the boy tomorrow."

His eyes searched my face wildly. They were naked and unguarded, and for an instant I saw the frantic, groping dismay in them. Then his face became cold and blank, and his twisted mouth broke out with a mirthless cackle.

"You're very funny," he said, cackling louder. "You're just about as funny as some of those jokes you send me. I'm laughing. Listen to me, Sidney. You're a scream—"

"I saw the marriage license, Harvey."

"Tell me more!" His voice became shrill.

"People are watching us. Please."

"Make me laugh some more!"

"You're nervous and edgy. You didn't sleep well."

"Sleep well? I have no reason not to sleep well, do I? While I'm asleep, and my back is turned to the mattress, the world is not busy telling lies about me. I don't have a willful and ungrateful sister who pays me back with heartache for all I've done for her, do I, Sidney?" His pudgy face was quivering. "Why shouldn't I sleep well when I know that I have Sidney Wallace to take care of everything for me? He can do anything! He can even come to me with brilliant stories!"

"I've done everything I—"

"Sleep is for fools, not famous men!" he shouted. "Stop snoring, Sidney!"

I sat there and allowed him to go on, the way a man does not bother to turn off the northeast wind, and when the waiter brought my dinner, and I borrowed my eyes back to look at the plate, Harvey's voice broke.

"Sidney—look at me—" There were tears in his eyes now. "I don't ask much of you, do I? Hunsecker gives, he doesn't take. Isn't that so?"

"Of course, Harvey."

"When Hunsecker asks for a favor there must be a very good reason."

"Of course, Harvey," I said.

He held his hands to his chest humbly. "Would I ask you to put an end to this terrible mistake between Susan and what's-his-name, the boy, if it wasn't important? I don't have to tell you, do I, how much it means to me that she doesn't do anything foolish with her life, that she doesn't throw it away on someone common and ordinary?"

"No, Harvey."

"I don't have to tell you, do I, how personally embarrassing it would be for me to become openly involved in such distasteful business? A man of Hunsecker's importance cannot place himself in a position where he is open to attack and ridicule from all who would humiliate him, can he, Sidney?"

I shook my head.

"I'm a tired man," he said, with the violins playing suddenly in his voice. "With one hand I seek the truth, and with the other I fight off the hungry wolf pack. Hunsecker is only human. He can take just so much punishment."

I glanced at him sharply. Such an admission was always an alert.

"I need a rest." He was taking out his wallet and extracting an envelope from it. "Peace and relaxation," he sighed softly.

He showed me the tickets. They were for the next sailing of the *Queen Mary*.

"You?"

"Let this country learn what it's like to be without Hunsecker for a while. A month without Hunsecker is better than a sick Hunsecker, isn't it?" The tears came back.

I had to look away.

"Hunsecker on the high seas," he breathed. "It will be good for everybody. But it will not be good for *me* unless I have peace of mind while I'm gone."

I couldn't wait any longer. I knew what the answer was, but I had to ask, to believe it with my own ears.

"Harvey"—I swallowed—"who—who is the other ticket for?"

He looked at me, dabbing at his eyes with a handkerchief. "She has never been to London or Paris. It will thrill her."

"Harvey—"

"I will surprise her with the tickets, and she will forget all the trivial unpleasantness that has come between us lately." His eyes brightened. "She will thank me for having opened her eyes to this foolish infatuation. She won' even remember the boy after two days at sea. I will introduce her to every great personage in Europe. She will know what it means to be the sister of Hunsecker. I am all she has in the world, and I want to do everything I can for her, Sidney."

I tried the iced coffee, but it choked me.

"She will like that, won't she?"

I shouldn't have allowed myself to look at his tense, white face.

"Won't she?"

I shouldn't have allowed myself to see written there how very much all this meant to him—and therefore to me. Because above the whooshing sound of the revolving door and the clatter of dishes and the babble of voices, I heard my own voice, speaking for some part of me that had always wanted far too much for me, and it was saying weakly, "All right, Harvey. All right. I'll try."

"Perhaps if you speak to the boy," Harvey said in a soft voice.

"I'll try."

"He may not be as headstrong as Susan."

"I'll try, Harvey," I said, feeling the sickness creeping into my stomach.

And then I felt a hand on my shoulder and a familiar voice saying, "Stop following me, Sidney," and I looked up to see Al Evans' face, no longer coldly suspicious but grinning now with approval.

"Al," I tried to warn him off with my eyes, but he stood there glancing at Hunsecker and then back to me—the very stupid, very suspicious Al Evans, standing there checking up, wanting to see things with his own eyes. Then he slid into the chair beside me.

"How are you, Mr. Hunsecker?"

Harvey lifted a glass of water to his mouth and said, "Sidney, who's your friend?"

I licked my dry lips. "Harvey, this is Al Evans, the agent."

Evans smiled expectantly.

"I'm very hard of hearing tonight," said Harvey, examining the glass of water. "I did not hear anyone invite your friend, Mr. Al Evans, the agent, to sit down at this table."

Evans' smile fro.. "I only—"

"Maybe my eyesight is failing," Harvey said, "and I did not see the sign over the door saying that this is a cafeteria."

Evans scrambled to his feet. "I'm awfully sorry, Mr. Hunsecker. I just wanted to say hello to Wallace here."

Harvey turned his pale eyes on him. "Why—Mr. Evans?"

"Well, you see—"

"Al," I said quickly, "I'll see you tomorrow. Okay, baby?"

"Sure," Evans said. "Sure." He started backing away.

"Well, good night, Mr. Hunsecker." He bumped into a waiter and then turned and fled.

"What about tomorrow?" Harvey asked me flatly. "What are you seeing him for tomorrow?"

"Business," I said. "You feel like dessert?"

"What kind of business?"

"He has clients who sometimes need publicity. That's all. How about some of that Dutch apple cake? I think I could go for that. How about you?"

"Which client, Sidney?"

"What's the difference? It's just dull business."

"I'm interested in dull business. Particularly if it's other people's business. For that they pay me money. What do they pay *you*, Sidney, for not answering questions?"

I looked at him for a long moment, and finally I said, "Herbie Temple."

Harvey stared back at me, the wheels going round and round. "Your client?"

"Not yet," I said.

"When?"

"Soon."

"How soon?"

I gave up. "Tomorrow."

He smiled—a slow, humorless smile. "That's nice, Sidney, I like to hear that you're doing well. It gives me pleasure." He extended his upturned palm to me. "Give me a dime."

"What for?"

"Give me a dime, Sidney."

I dug into my pocket and handed him the coin.

"I'll be right back," he said, sliding out from his seat. "I want to make a phone call—to the paper." He smiled at me, and I watched him walk away, past the gantlet of staring faces that greeted him wherever he went.

Do me something, I was muttering to myself in silent prayer. Please do me something that will allow me to wrench myself away from you in the white heat of anger while there is still time. I sat there muttering to myself and tearing at the bread crumbs and waiting for him. Finally I saw him coming back to the table, and I knew by the irritated look on his face that it had been too late for him to kill the item—too late for him, in this one instance, to make certain there would never be any payment before delivery as far as he and I were concerned.

He sat down at the table, slipping the smile back on. "Don't ever say that Hunsecker is ungrateful."

Oh, Lord, no, please. "Why not?"

"You said Herbie Temple will be your new client, didn't you? You want him to get off to a good start, don't you?"

I nodded dumbly.

"Hunsecker doesn't say thanks with the lips. Anyone can do that. Hunsecker likes to say thanks in a way that has meaning." He paused dramatically. "I have just phoned the paper and added something to tomorrow's column. Tomorrow Hunsecker will tell fifteen million people what a great performer Herbie Temple is. I am saying thanks, Sidney, for all you are about to do for me. Let me hear you say, 'you're welcome.' "

I stared down at my napkin. It was white and square, like a marriage license, like a ticket on the *Queen Mary*. I tore at the napkin but it would not give. I looked up at him. "I've got to be going now," I said.

"I'll meet you later at the Panamanian, then."

"No, Harvey. Stay away from the Panamanian tonight. I need elbow room. I want to be free. I want to be able to do whatever I have to do, whatever comes up."

He eyed me sharply. "You are concealing something from me, Sidney. Hunsecker likes to play open poker, no cards up the sleeve."

"You said you didn't want to be mixed up in any unpleasantness, didn't you?"

"I don't believe in unpleasantness. Unpleasantness is the last resort of the weak and helpless."

"All right, then," I said. "Relax. Don't ask questions. Go to Twenty-One, like you always do. Sit at your table and be happy and let people come to you and amuse you. If I need you for anything I'll call you. But I won't need you for anything."

If the act had to be done, it had to be done. He would never forgive me if I made him a party to my deeds by telling him of them beforehand.

"You're beginning to sound like a man who knows what he is doing, Sidney. Wonders will never cease."

"I'll try," I said. "That's all I can do, is try."

His face darkened briefly. "You can do even better than that." He picked up the menu. "On your way out, see if you can find one of the Marx brothers for me."

I got up and walked away. The pains were stabbing at my insides, and I no longer could tell myself it was the heat. Because I knew now what I had somehow known all day . . . what must have been at the back of my mind from the moment of awakening: I was not going to be able to avoid using Harry Kello. I had gone through all the motions, but that's all they had been—motions. Some time that night, I would be calling Harry Kello, the unsmiling lieutenant of the Twenty-first Precinct.

IV

The papier-mâché palm trees and air-conditioned breezes were beginning to draw people in off the streets. Slowly the Panamanian was coming alive. I sat there at the table with the smoke in my nostrils and the music pounding at my ears, and watched Joe Robard sucking on the damp cigar while the wheels moved slowly in his brain. I watched the dark, heavy-set features peering at the dance team out on the floor through dull, expressionless eyes, and I waited for the face to reveal the inner decision.

Finally he took the cigar from his mouth and turned to me.

"One thing keeps bothering me," he said thickly. "You supposed to be working for *me,* and here I am being hung up to do favors for *you.* That I don't have to pay no hundred and fifty dollars a week for, Sidney. I don't need no press agent around here for Joe Robard doing his own spade work."

I shook my head impatiently. "Not for me, Joe—for Hunsecker. Is that bad, to be doing a favor for Hunsecker? Is that any different than doing a favor for yourself?"

He examined me carefully through the smoke screen

of his cigar. "You sure the only reason you want me to
see this boy Dallas tonight is because Hunsecker gonna
like me for showing interest in the guy his sister gonna
marry?"

"Not just interest, Joe. It's much more than that. It's
interest in the boy at a time when others are turning
their backs on him just because of idle rumors in the
papers. That takes real courage, the kind of courage that
Hunsecker can appreciate. To step forward with a vote
of confidence, someone as important as you are, Joe."

He nodded, grunting with pleasure. "But how do I
know these things about the boy I hear all day"—he
waved his hand vaguely—"how do I know they ain't
true?"

"A man is always innocent until proved guilty," I
said. "And remember, all I want you to do is have a talk
with him here tonight. Just sit down and discuss things
with him and then, at a later date, we'll talk further
about the advisability of booking him into the club. You
complain to me all the time that I don't get you the kind
of publicity that fills tables. All right. Here's a golden
opportunity to help me get Hunsecker to love you up in
his column for months to come. That's a real pay-off,
Joe. That's money in the bank."

"Minus a hundred and fifty dollars a week for—how
many months is it?"

He was slipping away. "I'll tell you what," I said
quickly, "if it doesn't work out right, if you're dissatisfied
with the results, I'm off the payroll as of today."

That did it.

"The price is right," he said. "What do I do?"

"Right now, nothing." I jumped up. "Just sit tight
here while I try to locate the boy."

My office at the Panaman in was a windowless closet,
but it had a telephone, and it had a door that could be
shut without completely banishing the music that somehow always made my night work seem like play. Tonight
I could hear the music, but I knew I wasn't playing.

I gave the switchboard operator the number and
lighted a cigarette. Soon I heard the dull, worn-out voice
of Irving Spahn saying, "What is it?"

"Irv, baby, listen to me." I spoke rapidly. "Be as angry at me as you want. It doesn't hurt me. I know you don't really mean it. Be as—"

"What is it? I'm tired."

"I've been speaking to Joe Robard here. I want to do whatever I can for you, Irv. I'm going to show you how wrong you are. It seems Robard is definitely interested in Dallas. He feels there is a strong possibility he can show-case the boy at the Panamanian the way he did with Sinatra and Como, and you know what that did. It only made them what they are today. I want you to stop being stubborn, Irv, and get in touch with the boy and have him come over here tonight to speak to Robard as quickly as possible. I've worked for this, and I don't want Robard to change his mind about it."

"Sidney," he said without feeling, "I don't believe you."

"Some day a car is going to come at you, and you won't believe it's a car, and you'll be killed; that's where your stubbornness and suspicion will get you."

"I don't believe a word of it. How do you like that?"

"You want me to have Robard call you personally—right now? Would that possibly knock some sense into your head?"

His voice sat up in bed a little. "What?"

"I said, will it convince your highness if I have Robard call you in person?"

He didn't answer right away. "Sidney, I'm a tired man. I've had all I can take. If you're pulling another—"

"Don't say another word, baby. Just keep the phone clear for a few minutes."

I hung up quickly and went back to the table, to Joe Robard.

"You've got to call his agent," I said.

"Agents? What do I want with agents?"

I took him by the arm and gently pressured him to a standing position. "Please, Joe," I said, "just call Irving Spahn at this number"—I gave it to him—"and tell him to have the boy here to see you as soon as possible tonight. Don't let him pump you. Just tell him to deliver his client."

Robard grunted acknowledgment.

"And remember, Joe, you don't want the agent to come

along. You're not talking dough with the boy. You just want to have a chat with him. Have the boy come alone."

"A pleasure," Robard said. "If I never see another agent again, I'll live through it."

He walked to his office, mouthing his cigar, a lumbering bear of a man doing his little bit to keep his night club from losing more money than its competitors.

I waited at the table, listening to the dark-haired Latin on the floor fighting the microphone with his tenor voice, and in a few minutes Joe Robard came back and sat down.

"Your friend, the agent, is an excitable man. He should go to a head doctor."

"Well? Well?"

Robard turned his heavy lids on me. "The Romeo with the voice will be here by ten o'clock. Joe Robard will charm him up to the eyeballs."

I squeezed his arm. "Thanks, Joe."

He regarded me shrewdly. "What you thanking me for? I ain't doing it for you, I'm doing it for myself. Remember?"

"That's the spirit," I said, getting up. "Now I've got to get back to work. Let me have a chat with him first when he arrives. Then I'll introduce you. Okay?"

"You're the boss, Sidney. Me, I'm only the press agent tonight. I only wish I was making the hundred and fifty a week that goes with it." A laugh rumbled in his throat. "But I guess I ain't got your talent. Lots of times I say to myself, 'Now Sidney—*there's* a man of talent. What wonders he could of accomplished if he used all this talent to do something worthwhile!"

It wasn't often that Joe Robard was funny enough to get two laughs in a row from himself. This was a memorable night in all kinds of ways.

I went out to the hat-check room in search of Selena Green. The prices you paid for her cigarettes and favors seemed exhorbitant only until she got close to you and spoke to you with her body. After her, I'd have to get on the phone and locate Harry Kello.

Steve Dallas stood in the archway for a moment, searching the room. Then he spotted me at the table and came down the stairs. He looked a little pale beneath his sun tan.

I reached out a hand. "Glad to see you, kid. Glad you could make it."

He thought about the hand for a moment, decided not to take it.

"Sit down," I said. "Joe Robard will be free in a little while."

He glanced at his wrist watch and slid into a chair uneasily.

"Not long," I said, watching him. More than ever I was struck by his boyishness, by the deceptive quality of seeming helplessness, the quality that got the women. The voice was just so much velvet.

The waiter eased over.

"Another old-fashioned," I told him. "What'll you have, kid?"

"Nothing," he said in an icy tone, inspecting the room so that he wouldn't have to look at me. The chill was on, all right.

"Susan told me the good news," I said.

He looked at me in surprise.

"About tomorrow," I said. "Congratulations."

He didn't know what to say. I helped him along.

"I want you to know how happy I am, kid. If there's anything I can do . . ."

The ice began to melt as he examined my face in bewilderment. "Gee, Wallace, I don't know what—"

"I know there's been a lot of misunderstanding on the part of a lot of people. Everybody makes mistakes. You do. Irv Spahn does. Hunsecker does. Who knows, maybe even I do."

"I don't know what to say."

"But everything worthwhile always works out all right in the end," I continued. "The Panamanian could very well be the start of real big things for you, Steve."

He ran a hand through his crew cut. "Lord, how I hope so."

"And if you don't mind, I'd like you to regard it as a wedding present from me."

His face broke into an awkward smile. "You're making me feel like an awful louse, Wallace."

"The present is not just for you. It's for Susan too."

He laughed. "On behalf of both of us, I thank you."

"Forget it," I said.

"Y'know"—he fumbled for words—"maybe I've been a little too harsh in some of the things I've said—"

"Gimme a cigarette and shut up," I said, smiling.

He brought out a pack. We both took one and lighted up.

I blew smoke at him. "I suppose you're planning on going away for a few days. A Broadway-type honeymoon."

"Well, as a matter of fact, that's the first thing I thought about when Irv told me about this Panamanian deal." He looked at me, and there was the kind of worry in his soft blue eyes that was the worry of a boy in love. "If Robard should want me to start right away—well, gee, I wouldn't know what to say."

"Don't worry about it," I said. "Joe is a slow man to make up his mind. And when he does, he usually likes a week or two for me to blow the bugles to herald the event."

"That would be wonderful," Dallas said. "I'd be a real heel if I didn't take Susie away for a while. I almost feel like I've never been alone with her. Gee, she's a great kid, isn't she?" His eyes were aglow.

"The best," I said, looking away. "Wait here. I'll go find the boss man."

I left him there at the table and went through the archway to the foyer.

"Lord Tarletons," I said to Selena Green. "Get rid of the others."

She shivered. She didn't have enough clothes on, and the club was overdoing the air conditioning. "Mr. Wallace . . . I . . . I'm afraid."

"I didn't hear you." I said. "Hurry." I poked my head in Joe Robard's office and said, "Five minutes okay with you?"

"You're the boss, Sidney."

"In five minutes, then."

I had to stop at the bar. I poured a double whisky down fast, and my hand shook when I signed the tab.

Steve Dallas was watching the floor show when I returned to the table. He was far off somewhere, lost in his own private dream.

"Well, what do you think?" I asked him. "You think you're going to like working in this room?"

He turned to me. "I'm walking on air already."

"You call this air? This is atmosphere." I mocked a choking cough. "And I don't help it one bit." I reached over and took the cigarettes, struggling to draw one out as I watched Selena working her way toward us past the crowded tables. My hands were shaking, and the pack fell right into my Old-fashioned.

"Damn!" I held up the soggy, dripping mess.

"That's all right." Dallas laughed.

"Oh, honey—" I signaled Selena. "You got Lord Tarletons?"

"For you, anything, Mr. Wallace."

Her hand, as I took the pack from her, was icy.

"Mmmm, you smell good, honey." I gave her a dollar bill. "Keep the change, and buy yourself another quart of the same perfume."

"Oh, you—" She pouted a nervous smile and walked away.

I worked open the left side of the pack. "I spoke to Robard," I said, drawing out a cigarette and tossing the pack to the kid. He put it away. "He'll see you in a couple of minutes."

"Swell." He glanced at his wrist watch. "I think I better make a call first."

"Ah-hah! Guess who." I laughed.

"Yeah." He got up smiling. "She's waiting for me. Talk about eager brides."

I went with him to the phone booth. "Does she know?"

"Know what?"

"About this? About the Panamanian?"

He smiled at me, eyes twinkling. "I tell Susie everything. She demands it."

"What did she say to the idea?" I asked, looking away.

He didn't answer for a moment. He didn't seem to want to.

"What did she say?" I asked him again.

"Oh, you know how women are," he shrugged. "She said she'll believe it when it happens." He stepped into the booth.

"Make it a quickie, kid. I'll wait here."

I watched him through the glass door as he talked with her, his face eager and alive with the future. Occasionally I could hear the peaks of enthusiasm in his voice. It was a voice that might have carried him to a kind of greatness in show business someday, if he hadn't made the mistake of crossing Harvey Hunsecker against the lights.

When he came out of the booth, beaming foolishly, I took him to Robard's office.

"Joe, this is Steve Dallas. Take good care of him now."

"It's my specialty," Robard chuckled.

"So long, kid." I held out my hand, and Dallas steadied it with his. "I guess I ought to say the best of everything."

"And I guess I ought to say *thanks* for everything."

"For nothing." I punched his arm and went out fast.

That was a picture I didn't want to have to remember for long—a slim, honey-haired boy with a soft voice and big, open eyes, standing there in the office saying thanks to me for nothing at all.

I blurred it as much as I could at the bar. Then I stopped at the telephone switchboard on my way out. "I may be back," I said to the girl, "if Mr. Hunsecker calls. I'm gone for the night to anyone else."

"Certainly."

Selena Green was in the foyer, shivering. I patted her bare arm.

"You're wonderful," I said.

"I've never been in any trouble, Mr. Wallace." Her teeth chattered. "There won't be any trouble, will there? I need this job."

"You need the fifty bucks, too, don't you?"

"Yes, but—"

"Then stop worrying. I told you, it's a practical joke. There won't be a thing to worry about. Now go on back in and get your mind off all this."

I went through the revolving door and gasped in the blast of hot clammy air that hit me. Harry Kello was already there, talking to the doorman at the curb. His two-hundred-and-fifty-pound body was a terrible burden on a night like this, and the sweat was pouring down his face. He walked over to me.

"Hello, Harry," I said.

"Sidney."

"Hot."

"Oh, boy."

I saw the other two men standing across the street, reading newspapers under the street light.

"How's the wife?" I asked.

"Fine," he said.

"The kids?"

"They're fine, too."

"Good," I said.

"How's Harvey?" he asked.

"So-so."

"Give him my regards."

"I sure will."

"Where you going?" he asked.

"An air-conditioned movie. It's too cold inside the club."

"It's plenty hot out here," he said.

"You won't have to stand it long," I said.

"How long?"

"Oh, not more than twenty minutes, I'd say."

"That's good," he said. "This is murder, this heat."

"Why don't you wait down the block a little?"

"What makes you think it's any cooler down the block?" He wiped his forehead with a massive paw.

"It isn't," I said, "but it might not look good in the papers. It's a little close right here, right in front of the place."

"Sure." He shrugged his huge shoulders and moved away. The men across the street looked up, saw him, and moved with him.

"So long, Harry."

"Give my regards to Harvey," he called back.

"I sure will."

"And thanks for the tip."

"Nothing at all."

"Maybe someday I can do *you* a favor."

"You never can tell," I said.

I walked away fast, like a man trying to run from his shadow. And when I got to the Broadway sector, I went into the Criterion Theater. I took a seat in the orchestra. I wanted to be downstairs. I wanted to be away from the smell of cigarette smoke.

V

I sat there for a couple of hours trying to lose myself in the picture. But it wasn't easy. The movie was about a boy and a girl in love. And when they clinched in the final fade-out, I stepped on other people's shoes in my haste to get up the aisle.

Outside, the passing hours had drained the streets of people, and I blinked in the brightness of the spectaculars that were still illuminating the hot sidewalks. In front of the theater, a newsboy was hawking the morning papers. I didn't bother with *The News* or *The Mirror*. I bought *The Globe* and scanned Hunsecker's column, just as though I hadn't seen it all in the proof. Then I tossed it away.

Broadway is one of those streets where it's light enough to read the morning papers in the middle of the night before, and there's a trash can on every corner to remind you to do so. As I walked uptown, I kept seeing the trash cans on the corners. I kept seeing the newspapers in those trash cans and the Broadway columns in those newspapers and the lives that revolved around those columns. As I walked uptown, I kept seeing trash cans filled with people. And it didn't make me feel any better to know that I had filled more trash cans than any press agent in town.

I went to Babe Scanlon's and sat at the bar—drinking without tasting the liquor, listening, but trying not to hear the drifts of conversation that floated by. It was almost one o'clock, but the place was crowded with people like myself, who never went home if there was still some place else to go. Home is where the music stops, the floor show ends, the lights go on, and you are only you again.

I gulped down the whisky, and the man in the seersucker suit and the loud voice at the other end of the bar kept on shaking a thick tongue at the bartender.

"—and I said to my secretary, Emily—tha's her name, Emily. Lovely girl, Emily—lousy secretary, lovely girl. I said to her, 'Betcha I know who they mean.' And when I told her, the tears come to her eyes. 'I don't believe it,' she said, 'I don't *believe* it.' So I said, 'You wait and see. Never wrong. Read the columns every day. Know 'em like a book.' So I said, 'You wait and see,' and I called it. Howdaya like that, Frankie? Called it on the *button*. *Right* on the schnozzola. . . . Lemme have this one on the rocks, with a li'l twist o' lemon peel. . ."

"The missus, she'll be surprised," the bartender said. "She used to listen to him on the radio and make a big fuss. Me, I don't go for the crooners. A ball game, or the weather reports. That's all. I'm not much for listenin' to the radio."

"Northwes' Mounted P'lice, tha's what it is." The man waved a finger. "Harry Kello always gets his man."

The bartender shook his head in awe. "Remember what he did to Tony Faye that night over on Third Avenue when Faye tried to pull a knife on him?"

"Ooooh!" The man in the seersucker jacket winced.

I drained my glass and threw some money down. "Doesn't he ever shut up?" I muttered to Frank.

"How do you mean?"

"Him." I motioned down the bar. "The one with the mouth."

"Oh. He was telling me about—"

"I know what he was telling you about."

"About this singer, this Steve Dallas fellow—"

"I said I *know*."

"Harry Kello and his boys picked him up a couple of hours ago. Everybody's talking about—"

"You're as bad as *he* is."

"Northwes' Mounted P'lice . . .," the guy said.

I slid off the stool and walked into the dining room, feeling sick. Herbie Temple was at the corner table with a whole crowd. He spotted me, and his face lighted up.

"Hey, Crosby! Bing Crosby! C'mere!" He must have seen the column already.

I went over to the table with careful steps. "The store is closed now," I said. "Tomorrow."

"Word for word," Temple said, holding up a circle of thumb and index finger. "I just want to bow humbly and eat every word I said today. How do you do it, sweetheart?"

"I fill trash cans with people," I said, and he blinked trying to make something of the bitterness in my voice.

The other people at the table looked at me blankly and went back to their conversations.

"Listen to this one," Temple said. "Maybe you can clean it up and give it to Hunsecker."

He went into a long one I had given Otis Elwell three months ago, and I stopped listening to him. I was listening to the vultures at the table working over the new carrion. They were all talking at the same time, and I was the only one who was really listening.

". . . and they weren't even *his*, at least not all of them. Marty saw some bridgework lying on the sidewalk. . . ."

"Jesus, three gorillas. Did they have to—?"

"Well, who told him to try putting up a fight?"

"Three of them . . ."

"Listen, you oughta be happy the police in this town . . ."

"I got three parking tickets last week. For my dough, I wish the kid would of killed them."

"I don't know. Frankly, I never had him tagged as the typ'."

"What—to try to outslug Harry Kello?"

"No, smoke reefers. But I guess you never can—"

"What does he have to try to get away for?"

"Maybe he had a late date. Ha ha."

"Don't be so—"

"The thing that kills me . . ."

"Sixty days, that's all he would of got."

"The thing that kills me . . ."

"When they take out the stitches, he'll look like embroidery."

"Will you *listen* to me for a minute!"

"I could've sworn butter would melt—"

"The thing that kills me is that he dares to holler 'frame.' "

"How can you be so sure?"

"Two years if he gets a day, I guarantee you."

"I'm telling you Marty Flynn was *right there*. He saw the *whole thing*. Right in the boy's *pocket*."

"Who says don't ever believe what you read in the columns?"

"Half of the pack was okay and the other half—marijuana. Yeah!"

"Did you ever try one?"

"Get away!"

"Wheee!"

"Well, what do you think, Wallace?"

"What?" I turned to Temple. He was tugging on my sleeve.

"You think it's a yock? You think he'll like it?"

I stared at him with unseeing eyes. "He'll love it," I said.

"I got more. Listen—"

I was walking away. "He'll eat it up."

"Wallace—"

"Give me another double," I said to the bartender. "Hurry."

I fished in my pocket for change. Suddenly, I had to talk to someone. I don't know why. I had to talk to someone. I downed the whisky in one searing gulp and went to the phone booth. I dropped a dime in, and then I was dialing her number. What if I did wake her? She had always awakened me, hadn't she? Hadn't she always come into the room and turned on the lights just to see if her little Michael was all right? What's the difference if it woke *me*, as long as the little one was all right?

Her phone came off the hook slowly and she groaned, "Yes?"

"Hello, Ma, this is Sidney."

"What—what is it?"

"Nothing, I just wanted to . . ."

"To what?"

To what? Yes, to what?

"I woke you, didn't I? I'm sorry, Ma."

"Of course you woke me. Decent people are in bed hours ago. I never heard of such—"

"Mike was right, Ma."

"Mike? What about Mike? My God, something's happened to Mike! Sidney, please!"

"No, no, nothing at all. I was only saying . . ."

"Oh, my God, for a moment—"

"Mike was right. He was right—"

"You're drunk, Sidney, aren't you?"

"Never get drunk."

"You've been drinking again, and you wake me out of a sound sleep to say nothing at all. You have absolutely no consideration—"

"Ma, listen—"

"I should think you would want to hide it from me in shame instead of calling me at this hour just to—"

I hung up quietly. Whatever had made me think—? I had another dime. She answered on the first ring.

"Mary, honey."

"Who is—? Sidney! Good heavens!"

"I didn't wake you, baby, did I?"

She laughed. "Oh, no, don't be silly, sweetie. I'm doing my nails. And what if you had? There's no one I'd rather—"

"I'm at Scanlon's. Meet me. I'll wait here."

"Now? Darling, you're mad."

"Please, Mary, please."

"But I'm all undressed. My hair is in curlers. I can't, really."

"Baby, I want to see you. I want to talk to you. I've got to talk. It's—"

"What's the matter?" she asked quickly. "Is anything wrong?"

"No," I blurted out, "nothing's wrong. But . . . but . . ."

"What, darling, what?"

"Can't you get dressed and come out? I want to sit and talk. This weather. I don't know. I just don't feel like being alone. . . ."

"Oh, darling, why didn't you call earlier? We could have had dinner together. We could have been together all evening. Why didn't you, Sidney? Why do you call now, when it's too late?"

"Is it . . . is it really too late?"

"Of course it is, dear." She sighed reluctantly.

"I suppose it is," I said slowly. The day was over. The night had ended. This day, this night, could never be undone. There was really no going back now and changing it.

"Sidney . . ."

"Yes?"

"I'm so glad you called. It was sweet and nice. I'll sleep

now and have pleasant dreams. I was worried—about today. About what happened."

"I'm sorry, Mary," I said.

"No, it was my fault. I shouldn't have said—"

"I'm sorry. Good night, Mary. I'm sorry about everything."

"Don't talk that way, darling," she said. "We'll make up for it. We'll start tomorrow."

"Yes," I mumbled, "tomorrow."

"Good night, darling."

I hung up slowly. Tomorrow. Everything tomorrow . . .

One of the captains was rapping on the door of the booth. I let him rap. I just sat there without looking at him. Finally, he pushed open the door.

"There's a call for you, Mr. Wallace."

I followed him inside to the reservation desk and picked up the phone. It was the switchboard operator at the Panamanian.

"Oh, Mr. Wallace, I've been looking for you all over town."

"What is it?"

"Well, Mr. Hunsecker called a while ago. He wants you to meet him at two o'clock."

"At Twenty-One?"

"No. His home."

The faint odor of caution. "What for?"

"He didn't say, Mr. Wallace."

Couldn't he wait? This was no time for taking bows, for the delicate staking of claims. Couldn't he wait until tomorrow?

"And Mr. Robard is terribly upset about something, and he said if I reached you he wanted to speak to you."

"Tomorrow," I said.

"But he said specifically—"

"I'll speak to him tomorrow."

"And a Mr. Spahn called several times. He sounded very peculiar. As though he was—"

"Tell me about it tomorrow!" I hung up, and went out to look for a cab.

Driving through the park toward Hunsecker's apartment, I gazed out of the window at the dimly seen figures sprawled on the grass in search of air to sleep in. Here and there, on the benches near the road, lovers were locked in sweaty embrace.

I was tired, and I closed my eyes.

But I still kept seeing the lovers on the benches, and they were all Steve Dallas and Susan Hunsecker.

"Let's get out of the park," I said to the driver. "Go up Fifth."

"Much nicer this way."

"I said let's get out of the park."

"Sure, if you're in a hurry, mister. I didn't know—"

But there was no hurry, really. There'd never be any real hurry again. The days of hurry were over. I had graduated, tonight. From now on, all I'd be doing was collecting the diploma—over and over again, seven days a week, all editions—with an advance look at the proofs. And I should have been feeling damned good about it, but I wasn't. That was going to have to wait until to-morrow, too.

VI

As I went up in the elevator to the nineteenth floor, old fears began to gnaw at my insides, prodded by bitter memories.

Nikko opened the door, blinking sleepy eyes.

"Which room?" I asked, as I went in.

"Mr. Wallace expected?"

"Of course I'm expected."

And please note, I come bearing no column copy, no apple for the teacher.

"Not home yet. Mr. Wallace wait? In the living room, please?" It was more of a command than an invitation.

I walked into the huge, thickly carpeted show place that Hunsecker called a living room, past the statuettes and golfing trophies that stood on the table in silent tribute to the man's self-love, and I sank exhausted into the green club chair. The lights were dim. The Capehart in the corner was playing softly, and as I sat there gazing at the portrait of Hunsecker on the wall, my eyes slowly closed, and I allowed the soothing music and the muted sounds of the city and the rich, sweet smell of success that permeated the room to lull my senses. I breathed the smell deeply, memorizing the scent, and then all at once I became aware of other sounds, other perfumes, and I turned, startled, as I heard her saying quietly, "You're early, Sidney."

"Susan!" I struggled to my feet. The fool! Why hadn't he made it at Twenty-One?

"That's right . . . Susan," she said, curling up on the sofa and watching me carefully. She had on pink lounging pajamas, and she looked older, much older than when I had seen her in the office earlier in the day.

"You—you're up late." I looked around nervously. Why the *hell* hadn't he made it at Twenty-One?

"Harvey said you'd be here," she said, eyeing me closely. "He said I should try to be up when he got home."

I swallowed.

"He said he wanted to have a little chat with me, Sidney. He wouldn't tell me what about." She paused. "Do *you* have any idea what it might be about?"

So it wasn't to be a victory council, after all. It was to be something far worse. . . .

"How should I know?" I said thickly, sinking back into the chair where I would not have to look at her face if I didn't want to.

"I just thought you might."

I loosened my tie and opened my collar.

In the half light, it seemed as though she had too much powder on her face, and her eyes looked strange, as though she might have been crying, or drinking, and I had the feeling suddenly that she was watching me too intently.

I took off my jacket and folded it on the arm of the chair. "Can Nikko fix me a drink?"

"Nikko's gone to bed. What would you like?"

"Never mind. It isn't—"

"What would you like?"

"Bourbon and soda."

She uncurled herself from the sofa and walked past me to the kitchen.

"Not too much soda," I called after her.

I looked at my watch. Quarter to two. Much too early. I had been too eager, that was the trouble. Without meaning to, I had already started to press. I had arrived early, and the minutes were going to be knives of torment. I looked up, staring at the face on the wall. It had been captured on canvas by an artist who had managed to see only the strength and none of the weakness. It was the face of the man who had won power and fortune, not of the man who had summoned me to this room tonight because he felt unable to face his sister alone.

She came in noiselessly. "Here you are."

I jumped, taking the drink from her with a shaking hand.

"What's the matter, Sidney?"

"What do you mean?"

"You're not nervous, are you?"

"Why should I be nervous?"

"I don't know. Do you?"

I noticed the glass in her hand as she sat down on the sofa.

"Since when do you . . .?" I nodded at the glass.

"Why not? I'm a big girl now. I'm even big enough to get married. Don't you remember? It's tomorrow." Her voice did funny things. She raised her glass. "Cheers."

"Cheers," I said, gulping down the whisky gratefully.

"Why don't you look at me, Sidney?"

I turned to her. "Okay," I said, "I'm looking at you." I held her gaze for a moment, and then I had to drop my eyes. "You look cool," I said.

"And you look nervous."

I finished the drink.

"What are you nervous about? You're not getting married. It's me. Look at me, Sidney." Her voice rose. "Tell me, do I look nervous? Do I look like a girl who is going to get married tomorrow? Am I all dewy-eyed and flushed and breathless with excitement? Look at me."

I glanced hastily at my watch. Where the hell *was* he?

"I know why you won't look at me," she said. "You're angry because I haven't thanked you yet."

I stared at her. "Thanked me?"

"Yes. For being so nice to Steve, for getting him that wonderful engagement at the Panamanian. He did get it, didn't he?"

"I—" My voice stuck in my throat.

"It's been so many hours since I've heard from him.

He never called me back, as he said he would. I guess he was so excited he forgot all about it. Isn't that terrible? Sleeping Beauty, who can't sleep because of the heat, and Prince Charming, who hasn't even called about rescuing her. He did get the job, didn't he, Sidney?"

I swallowed. "I don't know."

"You don't know? That's very strange. Didn't you arrange it? If you don't know, who *would* know? Of course, Steve would know, but he doesn't seem to be talking, does he?"

"I . . . I left him at the club." I squirmed in the chair. "I . . . I had to leave."

"Oh, you had to leave? Then you weren't there when he talked with Mr. Robard."

"No." I wiped my forehead with a handkerchief.

"And you weren't there when he left?"

I shook my head.

"That's too bad," she said.

"What do you mean, too bad?" I cried out.

"Well, if you hadn't left when you did, you would have known whether Steve got the job. You would have known everything there is to know, and we wouldn't have to be sitting here playing guessing games. Let's play another guessing game, Sidney. Or don't you like guessing games? Let's try to figure out where Steve might be right now, shall we?"

"Look," I pleaded, "can't we just sit here and wait for Harvey? I'm hot and tired."

"Maybe you work too hard, Sidney." She got up and came toward me. "Maybe you're cursed with too much ambition."

I twisted away, groaning, "Give me another drink."

"Maybe you're too intent on finishing whatever you set out to do."

"Please. I'm tired." I struggled to my feet and went to the window to escape the sound of her voice.

"What do you think of Bermuda for a honeymoon? Or don't you know about such things?"

The lights of Long Island twinkled across the river.

"Steve loves to swim and go sailing. He loves the hot sun and clear blue skies. Isn't it wonderful when two people who love each other turn out to like the same things, too?" Her voice was winding up too tightly. "It even turns out that we both always wanted nothing but a very small wedding. We always wanted—oh, God, all the things we wanted!"

An airport beacon flared and swung away in the distance.

"Did you ever want something too desperately, Sidney?" I clung to the window.

"The worst thing in the world," she choked, "wanting something so terribly, awfully much—" She broke off.

And in the silence I was aware, suddenly, of a change in the room behind me. The music had stopped. A voice was talking now. The announcer was saying something about five minutes of the latest news.

The latest news!

I turned and went for the radio.

"Wait a minute!" Her voice stopped me. "What are you doing?"

"You don't want to hear this," I said.

"Why not?"

"I'll get some music."

"What's wrong with the news?"

"No!"

"What's wrong with the news, Sidney?"

"I don't want to hear it," I said thickly.

"Aren't you afraid you'll miss something important?"

"I'll read about it tomorrow."

"Sidney!" she cried out in a terrible voice. "Do you really think that I don't *know?*"

I stared at the crumbling face.

"Don't you know there was a one-o'clock news and a twelve-o'clock news?" she cried harshly, coming towards me. "Don't you know Steve is important enough to make *all* the news? Didn't I tell you that he's the most important man in the world? Didn't I, Sidney?"

I backed away, knowing there was something to say, but I was too tired. I needed sleep. Eight hours of forgetfulness. Tomorrow would be different. Where the hell was Harvey?

"Listen to the news!" she was screaming. "Stand there and let me look at you while you listen to it!"

"Don't, Susan!" I held up a hand weakly.

"I just want to see your face! Listen to the news!"

Her face was close to mine. The voice of the announcer was forcing the words on my protesting ears, the whole story, the details. . . .

"Listen!"

Her eyes were bloodshot. She *had* been crying. She looked old. Just like I felt. Old and tired. Too much to drink. It didn't make you forget. Just made you tired.

"It makes you tired," I mumbled brokenly. "You shouldn't drink, Susan. It makes you say things."

The voice on the radio had gone on to other news. But the face wouldn't go away.

"Thank you," it shrieked, "for saving me! You saved me from marrying a dope fiend! Thank you!"

"Please, don't!"

"Thanks, Sidney!" She broke into a hopeless wail, and fell on the sofa. "Thanks, thanks, thanks, Sidney. You're so good to me. You and Harvey were always so good to me. How can I ever thank you?" Her voice cried out in torture, "Steve . . . Steve . . . they were so good to us, Steve. . . ."

"Stop it, Susan," I groaned, sinking down heavily beside her. She was sobbing into the cushions, staining them with her tears.

"It won't be so bad," I said to her softly. "You can go away, take a trip somewhere, forget about all this."

Her body shook convulsively.

"You'll go away on a trip, see new faces. It won't mean a thing in a couple of weeks. Come now, stop crying. You'll go away on a trip with Harvey—"

She looked up at me slowly, still sobbing.

"—on the *Queen Mary*. Next week. He's got the tickets."

"No." Her tear-stained face was turned to me, and she was moaning weakly. "No. No."

"That's right," I said. "Next week. To Europe. On the *Queen Mary*. I saw the tickets."

"My—God—" she whispered softly. "No."

"Stop crying now. Just you and Harvey. You'll forget everything. That's a good girl. No crying."

She was suddenly quiet, just staring at me.

"Good girl, now." I patted her. "I'll get you a drink.

You'll feel better. I'll get us both a drink." I got up from the sofa, and her eyes followed me as though she were hypnotized.

"Wish I was going on a trip myself," I said. "Away from this city. Be right back. No crying, now."

I made my way to the kitchen and fumbled for the light. Hell of a place to keep his liquor, the kitchen. Surprised he didn't keep it in the safe. She'd have to drink nothing but Cokes until she learned the combination. Good brother, Harvey. Best brother a girl ever had. Not like me. Lousy brother. Mike was right.

The stuff burned going down. Not enough soda. No soda at all.

I went back to the living room with her drink. Nice and quiet now. Soft dance music. No sobbing. No Susan.

"Susan?"

The room was too damned big. No Susan. Only the stains on the sofa.

I fell back in the club chair and drained her drink. If that's the way she wanted it, it was okay with me. Let her stay in her own room where I couldn't hear her. Let her go jump in a lake of tears. Let her go jump—

I sat up as it came to me suddenly, compounded of small, unrelated things: the look last seen on the crumpled face; the whispered words; the silence of this room; the noise heard from down the hall; the scraping, squeaking sound—like—like what? Like a window—

Yes, like a window!

"Susan!" I was out of the chair and fighting my way across the endless stretch of living-room carpet to the hall, crying wildly, "Susan! Susan!"

I was moving too slowly, like a man in a dream. The fog was enveloping my brain. "Susan, wait!"

Her bedroom was dark. The window was open. "Susan! No!" I rushed to the sill.

"What is it?"

I wheeled around gasping, "Susan!"

Dimly, I saw her there on the bed.

"Thank God!" I closed the window and went to her. "What's the matter, Sidney?"

Her voice was under control now. She'd be all right. But that open window—

"What are you doing there?" I struggled for breath.

"Thinking," she said quietly. "I've been lying here thinking."

"Well, come on," I said in a shaking voice. "Get your drink."

She sat up on the bed slowly, her eyes boring at me through the darkness. "So you thought I would kill myself, Sidney. Is that what's expected of me?" She got up and switched on the lights and stood there staring at me. "You don't know me any better than that?"

Her eyes were dry now, and the last drop of heartbreak had been wrung from her voice, leaving it cold.

"I was afraid for you, Susan. You're upset."

"Afraid all your plans were going out the window?"

"Don't even say such a terrible thing."

As she stood there looking at me, a strange, cold light stole into her eyes.

"Yes," she said slowly, softly, "a terrible thing." Her eyes gleamed. "Wouldn't it be a terrible thing if everything were to go out the window?"

I went cold at the sound of her voice.

"You," she said, "and Harvey, and the innocent little girl he can't let go of." She smiled suddenly. "All of it out the window."

"What do you mean?"

She went past me toward the door.

"What a terrible, wonderful thing that would be." She was laughing.

"Susan!" I jumped to her side, but it was too late because the door was already closed, and she was turning the key in the lock, and I was tearing at her hands savagely, crying, "What's the idea?"

She broke away, with the key in her hand, and stood in the center of the room. "Come on, Sidney." She faced me defiantly. "Let's see you take it away from me like you've tried to take away everything else!"

I ran to the door and fought with the knob, but the door was locked. "Listen now"—I went to her and grabbed her wrists—"What do you think you're doing?" I tore at her fists and worked them open. The key was no longer in her hand.

"*Search* me, Sidney," she said quietly. "Take my clothes off. Maybe you'll find the key. Maybe you won't."

"What's come over you?" I cried in a hoarse voice.

She laughed, a horrible laugh, and ran to the switch, and suddenly the lights were out, and she was moving at me in the darkness, and her arms were encircling my neck, and she was murmuring, "Hold me close, Sidney. I want you to know what Steve will have to wait for. Kiss me, and find out what he's missing. Go on. Don't be afraid. Kiss me. Harvey isn't here yet."

"Stop it!" I fought to rip her arms from me, but she locked them tighter. "Susan!" She squirmed against me, smearing my face with her lipstick. "Don't be a fool!"

"This is what you wanted," her voice stabbed at me in the darkness. "This is what you've been moving heaven and earth for, isn't it, Sidney? You didn't want Steve to have me. You wanted me for yourself, didn't you? Isn't that the truth that Harvey will always believe?"

"My God! *No!*" I broke her grip and threw her away from me, and rushed to the wall and turned on the lights.

"Oh, yes, Sidney," she said quietly, smiling and nodding.

"You wouldn't!" My face blanched. I looked around frantically.

"The window, Sidney," she said in a voice of iron. "That's the only way out. But you won't take it. You don't want to die."

"Susan, please." I reached out a hand imploringly.

"You want to live, and grow fatter, until some day you'll be so fat with power, you'll be even greater than Harvey Hunsecker, isn't that right, Sidney? You don't want to die. You just want to live so you can kill!"

"You wouldn't lie to him."

"Of course I would," she said harshly. "The terrible thing about people like you is that decent people have to become so much like you in order to stop you—in order to survive." Her voice rang out. "But they always survive, Sidney! That's the wonderful thing."

"Give me that key," I said quickly.

"Steve will be out some day. It doesn't make any difference when. He'll be out, and I'll be there to meet him."

"I said *give me that key!*" I moved at her.

She backed away, crying, "But you're through, Sidney! You're as finished as a man can be while he's still alive!"

I grabbed her with one hand and slapped her face hard. "*Give* it to me, do you hear!"

"You came into her bedroom," she spit the words at me, "and you ruined the sister of Harvey Hunsecker forever. You destroyed the image, everything that's dear to him, didn't you, Sidney?"

"Shut up!" I struck her again.

"Let him live with the memory of what you're doing to me in this room for the rest of his life!" she cried out. "He'll love you for it!" She tore away from me and ripped the covers off the bed. "Come on, Sidney. Undress me and help yourself to the key!"

She stopped and turned to listen. I heard it, too. Outside. The noise. The front door . . .

"Susan," I moaned.

"Hurry, Sidney," she whispered.

"Oh, God . . ."

She was ripping her blouse into shreds, standing in her brassiere now and tearing at her trousers . . .

I went to her. "Don't!"

"You'll need the key, Sidney."

"Don't!"

"There, Sidney." She stepped back and the key lay there on the carpet, gleaming up at me, as the sounds grew louder—the searching voice, frantic footsteps. "You can go now," she said softly. "It's over—finished—done with—forever."

I picked the key up from the floor, moaning quietly to myself, "I'm sorry. I'm sorry . . ."

"I warned you, Sidney." Voices echoed out of the past.

"I'm sorry," I cried softly, as though they would ever hear me—any of them, all of them—to everyone I had ever known I cried, "I'm sorry," as I walked slowly to the door.

And then, as I knew I would, I heard her begin to cry out behind me. I heard the voice of a girl who would never be a girl again, and she was crying, "Help me, Harvey! Help me, Harvey! Oh, please, Harvey, help!" And from the other side, the other voice was shouting hoarsely and the furious fists were pounding against the door, and I went to it, moaning softly, "I'm sorry . . . I'm sorry," and I turned the key in the lock and pulled open the door.

And then I saw the face.

"Harvey. . . . Look, Harvey. . . . Wait a minute. . . . Listen to me. . . . Harvey. . . . For God's Sake! . . . Harvey! . . . Jesus! . . . *Don't* . . . ."

Tony Curtis portrays a Broadway press agent adept at the double cross.

Scenes from the Hecht-Hill-Lancaster movie, so starring Burt Lancaster and Tony Curtis, introducing Susan Harrison, and featuring Sam Levene, Marty Milner, Barbara Nichols and the Chico Hamilton Quintet. Produced by James Hill. Directed by Alexander Mackendrick. A United Artists release.

Hunsecker, powerful *New York Globe* columnist, is played by Burt Lancaster.

Kunsecker listens to his sister Susan, who wants him to approve her romance with a young entertainer

To help smash Susan Hunsecker's love affair, Sidney pressures a columnist and his wife.

Sidney whispers a smear item to a Hunsecker rival.

A cigarette girl becomes Sidney's unwilling accomplice.

Hunsecker holds court at his "Club 21" table.

Hunsecker blasts Susan's boy friend, while Susan looks on glumly.

Susan Hunsecker waits outside the stage door.

The Man Who Liked to Look at Women

First he glanced with deliberate unseeing eyes at some of the other passengers in the subway car who were, like himself, aging and work-weary and unbeautiful. Then he panned his gaze slowly across the advertising posters, reading—but not reading—of cough mixtures and hair rinses and headache powders. And finally, like a dog that has circled its bowl of food long enough, he looked directly at the girl, and she was unlawfully beautiful.

She was slender and bare-limbed and very blonde, and she wore a simple black dress and a glowing sun tan and the light of youth in her eyes. Lew stared at her above the page of his newspaper and something inside of him made him want to cry, and unaccountably he found himself thinking of the first time he had seen the Grand Canyon on the Greyhound Tour with Martha years ago, when he had felt the urge to jump over the edge.

Suddenly her eyes met his—cool, gray-green eyes—and he looked away quickly, thinking: you too, like all the rest of them ... cruel, thoughtless, selfish of your beauty. Impatiently he stared at the blur of print on his paper, and when he looked up at her again, he breathed imploringly: Please let me look at you for more than a few seconds—not furtively but with admiration. I want only to look at you, nothing more, as I would examine anything that is beautiful. Please let me. ...

But she wouldn't. She caught his glance immediately and forced it away, and then the train was at his station and he was out on the platform watching her disappear forever from his sight. It was so little that he asked for, really—and so unattainable: just to be able to look, that was all . . . without tension, without guilt, without the inevitable reprimand in their eyes. Take away summer sunsets and national parks and paintings that hang in museums, if they must, but let him enjoy the eighth wonder of the world.

He walked home slowly from the subway station, instead of taking the bus, and he was quiet at the dinner table, taking no part in the babble of his wife and the three children. And at precisely the moment he had known she would, Martha asked him if anything were wrong.

"Not a thing, dear," Lew assured her with a quick smile. "I guess I'm just a little bit tired."

And so much else, he thought.

"You've left some meat on your chops," Martha said, poking at his plate with her fork. "Look. All this here is meat. If you only knew how hard—"

"I'm sorry. I'll finish it," he said quietly. He gnawed on the bones and watched Martha across the table, telling himself again that he still had a deep affection for her, and wondering for the thousandth time whether his life would have been any different—one way or the other —if she had remained lovely to look at.

Afterwards, he listened while his eldest daughter, Tina, ran through her piano exercises, and when he saw Martha settle down in her chair with a pile of socks in her lap and the needle and thread in her hands, he put on his worn felt hat and announced that he was going out for a walk.

Martha looked up from her darning. "I thought you were tired?" she said evenly.

"Maybe the air will do me some good," Lew said.

"I see," Martha said to the heap of socks in her lap. She didn't say anything for a while, and then she added: "Will you bring me back an ice-cream cone, Lew?"

"All right," he said.

"Vanilla."

"Vanilla," Lew said.

He patted her on the head and left the apartment, but he did not go for a walk. He caught the bus to the subway station and rode downtown as far as Fiftieth Street and Broadway, and when he emerged to the street he crossed over and walked up to a brightly lit drugstore window. It was a balmy Indian summer night and the sidewalks were jammed with gay, pleasure-bound crowds. Lew stood there, bright-eyed, hardly knowing where to look first—a nondescript little man in neatly shabby clothes with his nose pressed up against the windowpane of the world.

. . . There were so many of them and each of them in her own individual way so wonderful to look at, but they walked too fast and there were too many places to look and only two eyes to see them with and almost before you saw them they were gone from your life forever and you wanted to shout "stop! stop!" and freeze the scene, like shutting off a motion-picture projector, but that would have been worse because so much of the beauty was sheer female movement . . . the sure-footed prance of long legs in high heels . . . the gentle up-and-down bobbing of long, shining hair on shoulders . . . the slow panther gait . . . the bouncy short steps . . . hips and arms and calves in a symphony of grace. . . .

He hardly noticed the redhead in the green dress who had stopped beside him to look at the drugstore window display. She stood there a long time without looking at him, and then after a while she gave him a short side glance and finally, with her face still turned to the window, she said: "When did you get back from Chicago, Mr. Wilson?"

He looked around, startled. "There must be some mistake," he said. "My name isn't Wilson. And I haven't been in Chicago."

"That's okay. Don't let it bother you," she said to the window. "I've met lots of guys who never were in Chicago, and they still liked to have a good time . . . Mr. Wilson."

"Look, my name is not—"

"I know," she turned from the window and smiled at him and he didn't like her face. "It's Jonathan Smith and you live in East Orange, New Jersey, and believe it or not you're waiting for a sidecar. I'm thirsty too. Shall we?"

"Shall we what?"

"Shall we dahnce?"

He looked at her mutely.

Her smile evaporated. "Am I boring you?"

"Please," Lew said, looking away.

"Well, then, what were you standing here for?" she said in a harsh voice.

Lew looked at her wildly, and then he turned and fled into the drugstore and ordered a small coke at the fountain, and it was several minutes before his hands stopped shaking. They just wouldn't let him, that was all. It was so little that he wanted of them and they just wouldn't let—

He sucked in his breath sharply. He hadn't seen the girl who was sitting diagonally to his right at the side of the fountain . . . the exquisite cameo face with shining gold hair piled high in a majestic upsweep. He set his glass down slowly on the counter and stared at her in rapt amazement. This was what he needed . . . as a drunk needs another shot . . . as a drowning man needs a straw. He began to examine the aesthetic wonder of her features, pleading silently: Please don't, please don't, pl—

She turned her head sharply and met his gaze head on, and he felt the impact in the pit of his stomach, and it was so sudden that he dared not avert his eyes too abruptly. And then after horribly eternal seconds he broke and looked down at his glass, feeling the color rising to his cheeks. He hated her. He hated every damned breath-taking one of them. But this one he hated more bitterly than any of them because she was right there now, hoarding herself like a beautiful miser, denying the cool, clear drink to the man who was dying of thirst. Well, she wouldn't get away with it, damn her. Not this time.

He looked up again, and her eyes were there waiting for him, waiting like a motorcycle cop behind a roadside bush, but he didn't care now. He stared boldly at her, without wavering, and he kept staring into her eyes even though his heart was beating uncomfortably fast, even

though the tension and the awareness of each other made
it impossible for him to derive any enjoyment from her
beauty. And finally she averted her eyes. Not he. *She* did.
But even as he was bringing his glass to his lips to cover
the flush of triumph, he became aware for the first time
of the large, florid-cheeked man in the loud sport jacket
sitting on the far side of the girl and obviously watching
him closely.

Lew tossed a dime on the counter and started to slide
from his stool, but he knew it was too late, for the big
man was already calling to him: "Is there anything I can
do for you, mister?"

Lew looked away as though he hadn't heard, but the
red-faced man got up from his seat, patted the girl com-
fortingly on the shoulder, and walked slowly towards
him, swaying slightly as he walked.

"You got something on your mind there, mister?" he
said, testily. "Something bothering you?"

Lew laughed nervously. "Why no," he said.

"Well, whaddaya looking at?" The man towered like
a mountain of over-dressed beef.

"I was only . . . only . . ." Lew groped for the right
words.

"You was only what?"

The big man stepped up to him and Lew could feel
heads turning to watch them, and he saw that the girl
had a scornful smile on her face and he could smell the
liquor on the man's breath. He felt terribly small.

"You was *what?*" the man with the loud jacket re-
peated.

"She's very lovely," Lew said suddenly, knowing even
as he said it that those were not the right words.

The big man drew in his breath sharply. "All right,
c'mon," he said.

Lew backed away slowly.

"Get moving," the big man said, his huge bulk shift-
ing forward implacably.

"Now wait a minute," Lew said hoarsely.

"C'mon. Come *on!*"

"Where do you get—?" Lew started to protest, but it
was too late because the big man was upon him now, and
somewhere in the terribly silent drugstore he heard a

snicker and he wanted to turn and run. But all at once a wave of hot, blind fury was surging over him and suddenly he was lashing out desperately with his fist at a thousand beautiful faces and a thousand pairs of accusing eyes and it caught the man hard in the pit of his stomach. And in the brief confusion as the big man toppled back stunned against the fountain, knocking over a glass, Lew turned and walked out as slowly as he dared and immediately was swallowed up in the crowds.

He didn't even turn to look back when he heard a voice shouting far behind him, but quickly went down into the subway station and took the local to Seventy-second Street and then changed to an express, and when he found himself standing near an exotic brunette with alabaster skin he pushed his way hurriedly into the next car and waited for the turmoil within him to subside. . . .

Martha was sitting in the big chair watching television when he got home. She looked up at him as he put his hat away, and the first thing she said was: "You forgot the ice-cream cone again, Lew."

"Oh, darn it, I'm sorry," he said. "Do you want me to go back down?"

"No. Never mind." She looked away.

"I'm sorry," Lew said again.

He walked into the bedroom, undoing his tie, and he really wasn't sorry, because he knew that Martha was more pleased with his having forgotten than she would have been with the ice-cream cone. That was the way it was with people. Everyone had a hidden source of pleasure. He sat down slowly on the edge of the bed and stared dully at his shoes.

Don't You Like It Out Here?

The trouble with Hollywood is, no matter how little there is to do at night, the sun is always there in the morning to make the hangover seem worse.

I swung around in the swivel chair, trying to work the glare down onto the trade-paper instead of smack into the hot coals I used for eyeballs, and I scanned the rest of the column. But I could have saved myself the eyestrain. We weren't in Connolly either. I tossed him into the over-flowing wastebasket along with Parsons and Hopper and stared gloomily at the junkpile on my desk.

"Is there anything wrong, Mr. Bliss?" my secretary asked.

I just gave her a sour laugh. One of these days I was going to surprise her and answer that question. I would take a few hours off and tell her what was wrong . . . with me . . . with everything . . . and she'd take it all down in shorthand and I'd sell it to the studio for a hundred thousand dollars—and that, of course, would turn it into a lie because then I'd be rich and a successful writer instead of a mediocre studio press agent going nowhere.

The phone rang, and I heard her say, "Right away," and then to me: "He wants to see you."

"That's sweet of him." I took my cashmere jacket from the back of the chair and walked upstairs to Producers Row to the office with the largest white shingle of all hanging down above it. Mrs. Samuels gave me the nod and I went right into the inner sanctum.

71

Finn Wildbeck, Norway's gift to Hollywood, sat slumped in the big wingback chair behind the enormous desk, and I had to look hard to find him. As though to add emphasis to the painful fact of his smallness, he seemed to prefer everything oversize—furniture, cigars, women. . . . I guess you would call it a form of masochism, like having his wife's picture on his desk where he'd have to see it.

He didn't bother to look up at me. He just waved a a hand at the chair beside the desk and muttered, "Sit down."

I sat, and I waited. Finally he turned the pale blue eyes on me and contemplated me for a long moment.

"Harry," he said, softly. His mouth drooped with gentle sadness. "Don't you like it out here?"

"Look, Mr. Wildbeck." I edged forward on the chair nervously. "It isn't my fault. I'm in there pitching. It's —it's—I don't know what it is with those columnists. They print whatever I give them about our productions, and the stars—even the little nothings on the lot—but when I try to feed them anything about you, I get all kinds of resistance. I'm beginning to think they—"

"My dear boy"—Wildbeck blinked at me with wounded surprise—"did *I* say anything? I only asked you, don't you like it out here." He took a deep suck on the cigar and unloosed a grayish cloud into the room. "In other words, Harry, I am inquiring do you enjoy the climate, and the convertible you drive, and the charge account at Dick Carroll's, and the steaks at Chasen's, and the wild rice at La Rue's?" He took another drag. "And do you enjoy the comparative ease of existence between the hours of ten and five within the gates of this studio?" He shot a glance at me. "Eh? What's that?"

I jumped. "Well sure," I nodded. "Yes, Mr. Wildbeck."

"Or do you hanker for the life you left behind as a reporter on that great New York newspaper—what is its name again?"

"It suspended publication many years ago," I said, looking away.

"Ah yes, yes, of course. Pity." He examined the tip of his cigar. "It is always a matter of great personal sadness to me to see men lose their jobs."

I swallowed the dryness in my mouth and stared down at my shoes.

Suddenly his voice rang out sharply. "Look at me, Harry. Quick. Look what I'm doing." My head jerked up and I saw him seize the framed photograph of his wife. "Now watch me." He opened the top drawer of his desk, placed the photograph inside and slid the drawer shut. "Symbolism, Harry, the way we do it in pictures. The flickering candle that goes out, to show death. The glowing embers that flare up into flame, then die out, to show the course of passion." He tapped the desk drawer. "What I have just shown you, in a traditionally artistic manner, is Mrs. Wildbeck, my wife, boarding the Super Chief next week for her annual trip to New York." His face broke into a smile that was devoid of humor. "How do you like that for imaginative symbolism, Harry? Perhaps I should have been a writer. Do *you* have a good imagination? You're young. There's still time for you to become a writer. You'd like that, wouldn't you—to graduate from what you are doing and become a writer for the studio?"

I swallowed. "Yes, Mr. Wildbeck," I said, in a stunned voice.

"All right, then." He sat up in his chair. "Come over here, next to me."

I went to his side and saw the stills there on his desk— Mickey Van Kroll's latest shots of the studio's current crop of stock girls, hopefuls who had come to Hollywood with large dreams, only to wind up inevitably as glorified models for bathing suit and evening gown layouts in the fan magazines. Wildbeck's pudgy hands were fondling the pictures like a poker player caressing a full house.

He began to deal them onto the desk one at a time. "Nothing," he grunted. The bathing-suit shot . . . the upside-down glamour shot . . . the all-American outdoor girl . . . the sweater stuff . . . "Nothing . . . nothing . . . nothing . . ." He dealt another. "Nothing," he said, then looked up at me to catch the expression that had suddenly hit my face. "Eh, Harry?"

"Jesus," I breathed softly, reaching down to pick up the glossy. "Who . . . ?" It was all so beautifully simple. Just a piece of black taffeta clinging to the body . . . the hair hanging carelessly, almost uncombed, to the bare shoulders . . . the teasing lighting, not enough of it, the kind that made your eyes strain to fill in details . . . and the face . . . lovely, but not smiling like the others . . . just sullen, to-hell-with-everybody sullen. She was magnificent. The caption said: "Rosemary Cobb." I glanced at Wildbeck. I saw his face and suddenly I was back to earth again and the sick feeling was taking root in me. I tossed the photo back on the desk and tried to shrug it off with the others. "Not bad—"

But he was already going into the speech. ". . . And the public is tired of the same old faces, Harry, just like you and I. They want new excitement, something to revive their fading interest. It is too long now since the studio has developed a new personality. . . ."

"A year," I said. "Laurie Sully."

Wildbeck waved his cigar in annoyance. "You should go far, Harry. You have a fine memory for trifles."

As though I could ever forget . . .

He cleared the phlegm from his throat and the memory of Laurie Sully with it. "Unfortunately for these young hopefuls, they are up against the cruel facts of life out here. In order to get the opportunity to prove themselves, they must know the right people and be liked by the right people, at the right time . . ."

Two years ago—poor, bewildered Susan Delacross. . . .

". . . But if that is the way things are, that is the way things are, and sometimes it is far more sensible to adapt oneself to life than to fight it." He tapped the photo with a well-manicured finger and breathed, "I think I would like to help this girl, Harry. She strikes me as having wonderful potentialities. Where are you going?"

I stopped, halfway to the door. I didn't have to hear the rest, really. I knew it all, right down to the chuckle and the tagline about discretion being the better part of valor, California community property laws being what they were. I turned, and our eyes locked.

"*I* understand, Mr. Wildbeck," I said.

"Then why don't you smile, Harry? Let me see you looking like a young man with a future."

"Yes, Mr. Wildbeck," I said in a hoarse voice, and went out fast.

I guess in any industry that numbered thousands of

decent, hard-working individuals, there always had to be a few people like Finn Wildbeck—and me. The amazing thing was, we always managed to find each other.

Personnel gave me a North Hollywood address and a telephone number. I called her on the private line, gave her a short spiel, and set up a luncheon date at the Derby.

She arrived five minutes early, and if it hadn't been for the hair—it was red, and down to here—I might not have recognized her. The loveliness was there all right, fresh-air, soap-and-water, early-to-bed loveliness. But the sullen, to-hell-with-everybody look had been strictly Van Kroll. She was only a kid, a bright-eyed, beautiful kid who would someday crowd Ava and Audrey right off the screen if she made the smart moves.

I grabbed my third martini at the bar, and a glass of sherry for her, and we took them to a table and gave the waiter something to worry about. Then I turned to her. "Why the look?"

"I was just wondering," she said. "I was wondering whether you drink that way because you're celebrating something, or because you're as hilariously happy out here as I am?"

"Look," I said quickly, "we didn't come here to talk about me."

The smile faded from her eyes, and I knew then that she hadn't wanted to come to the point so terribly soon. She snapped a breadstick nervously. "Okay, Mr. Bliss. You talk . . . I listen."

I clutched at my martini. "Well"—I took a swallow—"I really gave it to you all—at least most of what there is—over the phone. Finn Wildbeck is interested—"

"Finn Wildbeck?"

"—is interested in having you get a publicity buildup at the studio and I'm supposed to dig for the facts to get a campaign rolling."

She was eyeing me closely. "Why me?"

I laughed, but it didn't come off. "Well, you're not exactly what we call a monster, honey, and—and Wildbeck feels that you've shown sufficient promise as a motion picture personality to—to warrant going all out for you."

"Is that right?" She took her time lighting a cigarette. "And where, exactly, did I show this great promise?"

I looked for it somewhere in the martini glass and came up with an onion. "Your screen test," I said.

She stared at me for a moment. "You know something, Mr. Bliss?"

"You can call me Harry."

"You don't belong out here. You don't know how to lie worth a damn. The eyes move around a little too much and you duck behind that glass as though it were a mulberry bush." She blew a furious stream of smoke at me. "In the first place, my screen test wasn't just bad, it was awful. And in the second place, even if it had been good it wouldn't have made the least bit of difference with Finn Wildbeck because there's only one thing that makes any difference with Finn Wildbeck. Now do you want to talk straight, or must we go on playing games?"

I looked at her. I watched her trying to be as tough and hard as she talked. And I shrugged. "Okay, baby. You're so hep I won't have to draw diagrams then. I'll just put it this way: sometimes, in the picture business, you have to *know* the right people, and sometimes you have to *yes* the right people." I drained the martini down hurriedly. "Well, the time is now . . . the right people are Finn Wildbeck . . . and you, baby, happen to have been tagged 'it' . . . that is, if you want"—I waved a hand— "whatever it is that you want."

Her face went pale. "And . . . and where do you come in?" she asked in a faltering voice.

"Me? I'm the maker of myths. I establish the legend that you belong to *me*. We get seen in the right places. I whisper to the right people who whisper to the right columnists and presto . . . Rosemary Cobb and Harry Bliss have quote discovered each other unquote. That takes the curse off you. You can be seen in the company of Finn Wildbeck and me without Mrs. Wildbeck's gossipy friends getting the dangerous notion that I'm along merely as window-dressing. In fact, in some places you can be seen with Wildbeck without me, because after all, everybody knows that Rosemary Cobb and Harry Bliss are quote sharing the same soda-straw at Schwab's unquote."

She examined her cigarette for a long time. "And after that . . . ?"

I played with the silverware. I searched the crowded room desperately for the waiter and another martini. I shifted the knot of my tie. But she was still waiting for an answer. *And after that?*

"Look," I blurted out, "I don't write the script. I only dress the set."

She shook her head with a wry, bitter smile. "They must pay you an awful lot of money, Harry."

"Listen," I snapped, reddening, "you don't want it, say so, but don't give me any of that holier-than-thou routine. There are plenty more where you came from, and maybe you don't have what it takes anyway. A pretty face, sure, but it takes more than that. It takes a strong stomach, and if you just don't happen to have it—or want it—okay. It's a free country."

That got her.

"Who said anything about not wanting it?" she shot back in a voice that was charged with anger—anger for me, anger for the system, anger for not having been spared the opportunity to make the choice. "I'd be a fool not to want it, wouldn't I?"

"Suit yourself," I said.

"Wouldn't I be the prize sucker to let a Finn Wildbeck be too much for me after all I've gone through to get this far, which is just about nowhere at all?" She crushed out her cigarette as though it were a poisonous spider and fought back the bitter tears. "Can you imagine me getting a weak stomach now, after all those auditions for near-sighted, leg-crazy Broadway producers, and the months in the model agencies where only some of the girls were models, and the beauty pageants where the judges fought with each other to see who would handle the tape measure?" Her lips were quivering and I had to look away. "I was fifteen when I found out that sugar and spice and everything nice were *not* what little girls were made of—so just don't worry about me. Here I am, and there you are, and bring on Finn Wildbeck, wherever the hell *he* is!"

I raised the empty martini glass and looked her in the shoulder. "To you, honey," I said. "A big future."

"You're darned right," she said, swallowing hard.

And a little later, when I saw Leo Stern, one of Louella's legmen, heading for our table, I decided that now was as good a time as any to begin, so I said, "Smile, honey, quick," and took her hand in mine, and it was cold—cold like the hand of any kid who whistles in the dark.

Take it from me, there's only one way to be on the town with a girl in Hollywood. Take her on the merry-go-round, with the expense account paying for the rides, and don't strain yourselves reaching for the brass rings, because both of you are in it strictly for the angle and let the laughs fall where they may. Sure, it's the only way to do it, strictly for the angle and strictly for the kicks.

Sure.

Like the afternoon we picked four out of seven at Santa Anita and blew it all on the eighth because who needed the dough and who really cared, as long as the neighboring boxes were filled with blabbermouths who didn't need field glasses to spot red hair . . . and like the night I took her to the sneak preview at Riverside and we wrote "It stinks" on the card and didn't care that it was a Wildbeck production because we managed to laugh so hard that Hedda Hopper couldn't have missed seeing us even if the fruit-salad hat had slipped down over her eyes.

Oh, it was a great routine, and I'm sure that we didn't mind a minute of it. I guess all the terrible drinking was only because the night spots are smoky and the throat gets parched and you get an awful thirst.

We'd have dinner at Romanoff's and ringside at Ciro's and do a wobbly rhumba at the Crescendo and refuel in the Polo Lounge of the Beverly Hills Hotel and show ourselves at the Mocambo and some of the Sunset Strip joints whose neon by that time would be only a blur, and one night when we were halfway back to her apartment in North Hollywood I discovered that she was driving and I was reciting poetry and trying to recall the name of the last picture Susan Delacross had made before taking the sleeping pills, and when I woke up I was on the sofa in her living room with the morning sunshine in my face and a stiff neck and a velvet jacket on my tongue and my hundred-and-fifty-dollar suit looking like a rumpled potato sack, and the note on the table said: "There's some coffee in the Silex. If Benny Thau or Buddy Adler should call, I'm at Jax buying a new dress for the pace that kills."

But we made the *Hollywood Reporter* and *Daily Variety*.

We made them all.

How could we miss, with my know-how, her flaming red hair, and the Jax necklines? In fact, maybe my know-how had nothing to do with it.

I knew we were over the hump when people on the lot were using my first name who had never even known my last. And when we made Louella for the second time, I decided we could relax and take a breather for a night, so I took her to dinner in the quiet atmosphere of the Bel-Air Hotel.

The only trouble with that was, the crackling log fire was so convincing it made you think of places where it snowed in January, and that meant New York, which was home to both of us. And when you sit at one table for too long you find you can't keep the laughs going all the time and you can't just sit there and stare at each other, so you talk, and when you run out of gossip you talk about each other and it just doesn't seem like the time or the place for a lot of drinking. Maybe that was the trouble, too. That . . . and the talk about each other.

"Two of a kind, aren't we, Harry?" I could feel her eyes on me, as they had been all evening.

"Yeah," I muttered, watching the dancing flames in the fireplace, "aces back to back." And what I didn't say was: "And Wildbeck deals." I turned to meet her gaze. Every time I looked at her it was like coming upon her loveliness for the very first time. "You have to know what you want and go after it, kid," I said, too insistently, as though trying to convince myself as well as her. "It's the ones who don't know what they really want, or who know but don't know how to get it—*they're* the schnooks of the world. They're the ones who'll be paying the price of admission to see the pictures *you're* going to star in, and *I'm* going to write. Isn't that right?"

She looked away. "Of course."

"Sure, and they'll be sitting in the balcony, too," I said. "The squares . . . the cornballs . . . sitting in the balcony holding hands and waiting for the five-dollar raise to come through."

"But not us," she said to the fire.

"Hell, no. Not us." I doused my cigarette in the water glass. "Come on. Let's get out of here."

We drove most of the way back to her place in silence. It was warm, and I had the top down, and the sky full of blue-white diamonds looked almost as real as a studio backdrop.

The silence began to weigh too heavily.

"I bet it's snowing in New York right now," I said.

"I wonder," she breathed.

"Sure, we don't know how lucky we are. Just think, if we were in New York now we'd probably be cold and and wet and bundled up to our ears . . . probably sneezing and coughing, too. And look at us . . . with the top down."

I looked at us. I looked at her.

"We'd be riding in a subway or a bus . . . not a convertible," I said. I flicked my cigarette away and exhaled slowly. "Let's say we're married, you and I. We're probably just coming home from a neighborhood movie. Can't afford the big downtown houses because I'm just a hook-and-ladder chaser for one of the local papers and you . . . you're selling perfume behind a counter at Saks Fifth Avenue." I turned to her. "That's an awful thing—hiding those legs behind a counter—but I'm sorry, honey, we need the salary."

She smiled. I guess you would call it a smile.

I shifted into low speed at the foot of the hill for the long climb to the top where she lived, and I wondered whether Finn Wildbeck's car would make in high. "And instead of nearing your three large rooms and the balcony overlooking half of southern California, we'd merely be on our way to a one-room apartment in Washington Heights overlooking a nice brick wall and smelling of steam heat and your amateur cooking." I made the last hairpin turn. "And you know what I'm thinking right now as I sit in that bus or subway, shivering and coughing and sneezing? I'm thinking . . . just like a schnook of the world . . . I'm thinking I can't wait to get home, because I know there's some of that Italian salami from the corner delicatessen waiting for us in the refrigerator, and a couple of bottles of beer. And when we get through polishing that off we'll browse through the papers, tomorrow morning's papers, and read in the columns how many Hollywood marriages went on the rocks since the day before. And then we'll go to sleep, congratulating ourselves." I shuddered. "Pretty grim . . . pretty awful picture, huh, baby?"

The car crunched to a stop before the white stucco apartment house, and I turned to her in the darkness, trying to make out what was wrong with her face. I touched it with my hand and it was wet. "Ah, baby, come on now . . ." I sighed. It was wet and I kissed it suddenly. I kissed the wet cheeks and the trembling lips and I murmured gently, "Honey . . . baby . . . don't," feeling the ache inside of me.

"Harry," she breathed, with her head on my shoulder. "Oh, Harry . . . why did I ever have to meet you?"

"What a lousy bit of casting," I said softly.

"And why did you have to say Italian salami?"

"You love it too?"

"Terribly," she cried.

"The dry salami with all the garlic?"

"Yes," she wept, laughing.

"Ah, baby," I shook my head, "what a shame, what a shame."

"What'll we do, Harry?"

I took her face in my hands and looked into her eyes, her wet shining eyes, and there was so much that I might have said, but all I could say, "You know what you want, kid."

She stared back at me.

"Well, don't you?" I said. "You're almost there. You don't want to throw it away. . . ."

She twisted her face away from me with a little cry. I opened the door for her. "Good night, baby."

"Don't worry." Her voice broke as she scrambled out. "I won't get any lipstick on your career, if that's what you're afraid of."

Suddenly my hand shot out and grabbed her arm and I yanked her back into the car. "Whose career?" I snarled. And then my mouth was pressing cruelly on her lips so hard that she moaned with pain and the pain was what I wanted to hear and I dug my fingers into her back even harder as she fought to free herself. "Come on . . . say it . . . *whose* career?"

"Harry, don't—" she choked. "Please, Harry. . . . I'm sorry. . . ."

I let go of her. "That's all I wanted to hear."

She got out, sobbing, and ran up the steps, and I didn't even wait for the door to slam shut to drive away with a screech of tires, and I couldn't even think of going home. I had to stop at a bar on the Strip first. And I stayed there until the only pain I could feel was the ache in my head, and when I woke up in the morning it wasn't even morning any more, and when I got to the office the copy of weekly *Variety* was already there on my desk . . . the one that said: "L.A. to N.Y.—Mrs. Finn Wildbeck."

The call came from upstairs right after lunch.

"You can go right in, Mr. Bliss." Mrs. Samuels gave me the knowing smile.

"Well now, Harry. . . ." Wildbeck looked up at me with an expansive smile. "I haven't seen you in many days. You have been a busy man—a very busy man."

I ran my tongue over my dry lips and said nothing.

"Two things I have on my mind—both pleasant." He brought a flame to the tip of the dying cigar and I waited while he sucked it to life.

"Number one, it now appears as though we are not going to be able to get Elizabeth Taylor from Metro for *The Distant Years,* and the thought struck me, what a grand spot it would be to introduce this young girl, what is her name again?"

"Rosemary Cobb," I said, feeling the coldness growing in the pit of my stomach.

"Yes, yes, that's the one," he looked at me. "Of course, all this is still in the think stage. I would first have to decide that she is right for the role—naturally."

"Yes, Mr. Wildbeck," I said.

"Number two, I have spoken to Lerner Sprague, and I have convinced him that there is no reason why this studio cannot develop new writing talent much in the same manner as we develop fledgling stars. All of which means, the first opportunity comes along, in you go. Does that make you happy?"

I swallowed. "Yes, Mr. Wildbeck," I said.

I braced myself.

"Tell me, Harry, do you have any important social engagements the next few days or nights?"

I nodded hopelessly.

"Miss Cobb?"

"Yes," I said, in a hollow voice.

"That's too bad," he said. "Too bad. Now that I am, so to speak, alone for a while, I thought perhaps you might like to go to Palm Springs with me. We all of us here at the studio work too hard anyway, eh, Harry? But of course I wouldn't want you to break any important engagements. Too bad." He blew two perfect smoke rings at me. "Unless you would like to have her join us?"

I didn't answer him. What was the use of answering him?

"As a matter of fact," he drew cigar smoke into his mouth noisily, "it might give me a fine opportunity to evaluate the girl's personality at close range. Tomorrow—" he sighed. "It would be nice if you could arrange it for tomorrow. . . ."

I could arrange anything. I could arrange the second coming of Christ.

"We won't stay at the Racquet Club," he was murmuring. "Too crowded. So many picture people. There's a little place a few miles east of the Springs. La Jollita. You take your car and I'll take mine. Then we won't all have to go back in case you—or I—should get a hurry-up call from the studio. Neither of us is exempt from the urgent call of duty, eh, Harry?" His face cracked into a smile. "It could just be your good luck—or bad—that Lerner Sprague decides he wants to break you in on scripting the very day after you reach the Springs. Then where would we be—you and me and the girl—with only one car?"

I moved for the door. I had to get out into the air.

"Harry," his voice hardened, "I want you to arrange

it, do you hear me? I want you to call the girl. Come back here."

I returned to the desk.

"You can use my phone." He pointed to the private phone on his desk. "Call her," he said. "Do it now."

Dumbly I stared at the phone.

"Go on, Harry."

"Yes, Mr. Wildbeck."

I picked up the phone, and slowly I dialed the number. In a few days I was going to become a writer, and a girl who was only a beautiful kid was going to be started on her way to stardom, but I dialed the phone slowly, because in Hollywood good news never travels fast. And then I heard her voice.

"Hello, baby," I said. I stared down at the little man behind the desk, and somewhere inside of me I was crying.

"Oh, Harry, I was so afraid you'd never call again."

"Start packing, honey," I said to her. "We're going on a trip."

"Tell her not to forget the bathing suit," Wildbeck whispered, grinning.

"Where to?" She sounded far away.

"A little trip—" I faltered, looking at the face. I was looking at the grinning face and seeing everything there had ever been between us. I was seeing the years that lay in the past and the years that lay ahead for me, and maybe it was what I saw in that face. Maybe it was the sound of her voice saying again, "Where to, Harry?" Maybe it was a lot of things. Because suddenly I heard myself answering, "We're going where the snow flies, baby, and the Italian salami grows. Just you and me. Does that make any sense to you?"

"Oh, darling, yes, yes, what sense!" she was laughing and crying. "What beautiful, wonderful sense!"

"I'll pick you up in an hour."

I hung up and stood before the desk, feeling the wild happy pounding of my heart.

"What kind of double talk is that?" Wildbeck stared at me in bewilderment.

"She isn't going," I said, with a crazy little laugh.

The cigar stood still in his mouth. "What do you mean, she isn't going? Why not?"

"Because I told her not to," I said quietly.

He sprang to his feet, and his cheeks were mottled with rage. "Do you know what you're saying, Harry?"

I looked at the face and I knew then how badly I wanted no door left open. I did not want to be able to come back—not ever.

"I don't think she would have enjoyed herself in Palm Springs, Mr. Wildbeck, and I don't think she wants a future with a studio like this one. I've decided that I don't like the kind of pictures you make here, Mr. Wildbeck. They are without taste—like you, Mr. Wildbeck."

He came around the desk swiftly, fists clenched.

"Why . . . you . . ."

"Yes, Mr. Wildbeck?" I stood before him, waiting.

His hands fell to his sides. "After all I've done for you," he muttered harshly. "You were hungry . . . going nowhere . . . and I took you on . . ." He turned away. "I had such plans for you. The things I was going to do for you. Not just a writer. Big things." He sat down in the chair behind his desk and his voice became weary. "Sit down, Harry. I want to have a talk with you. You were always such a fool. I cannot bear to see you throw away everything for . . . for a girl . . . a nothing." He looked up at me. "That *is* it, isn't it?"

"That's right," I said. "A girl . . . a nothing."

"Now listen to me," he said softly.

I looked down at him and smelled forgiveness in the air, and suddenly I realized that he needed me, even now. All at once I saw that he had always needed me, that I had been, in a way, just as responsible for Finn Wildbeck as he had been for me. And knowing *that* would have to be part of the penance in the years to come, penance for a guilt that had been mutually shared.

"Sit down, Harry."

"I haven't time," I said. "I'm leaving, Mr. Wildbeck. Quitting."

His cheek began to twitch. "When?"

"Right now. As of this moment."

"You're fired," he said.

"I never liked the job," I said. "I want to find something clean . . . like spreading fertilizer."

"Get out," he said quietly.

"And I never liked the company I had to keep."

He jumped to his feet. "I said get *out!*"

"Quick, Mr. Wildbeck, look what I'm doing." I reached suddenly across the desk and ripped the cigar from his lips, leaving shreds of tobacco hanging from his stunned, open mouth. "Look!" I took the cigar and broke it in two. "Symbolism, Mr. Wildbeck, the way you do it in pictures. I have just shown you, in a traditionally artistic manner, the end of a beautiful friendship."

I tossed the broken pieces of cigar on the desk and headed for the door.

"Harry, you're through!" The voice came after me hoarsely. "You and the girl!" he screamed. "I swear before God that you and the girl will never get another job in pictures as long as I *live!* Do you understand what that means?"

I stopped at the door and turned to him, and I did not mind the words that came to my lips now, because I knew that they were there for the very last time.

I smiled.

"Yes, Mr. Wildbeck," I said.

The Way Men Are

The faraway noises of midtown Manhattan getting ready for another Saturday night drifted up the twenty stories and intruded in the half-dark, paper-littered office like muted jazz music in a morgue.

Al sat slumped at his desk for the last time, a slim, dark-haired man in his early thirties, with his desk drawers picked clean and five years of hopes and dreams and memories piled high in the wastebasket at his feet.

He looked up as Kennedy walked in briskly and stuck out his hand.

"Well . . . all the luck in the world, Al," Kennedy said. "Keep in touch, will you?"

"Thanks," Al said, taking the hand. "I sure will."

The hell he would.

Kennedy avoided his eyes. "And I want you to feel that if the new job doesn't pan out, your old desk will always be waiting for you."

"Thanks," Al said. Kennedy didn't mean a word of it, and he knew that Al knew it, but that was all right. It was part of the ritual.

Kennedy's heels clicked down the hall to the elevator, and then Al was alone with the distant music of the streets, and his crowding thoughts—and Hilda.

He could hear her puttering around in Kennedy's office, doing all the unnecessary little things that were so necessary to her because they delayed her inevitable journey uptown to a lonely dinner—and the gay, romantic evening that happened only to other girls.

"Hey, Hilda," Al stared vacantly out of the window at

the lights in the tall buildings. "Don't you ever go home? It's twenty after six."

"Don't be silly," she sang out. "I love it here. I pay Mr. Kennedy to let me work overtime. You poor thing. I'll bet you're sorry you're leaving."

"Yeah," he said, hurling a paper clip hard against the wall. "You said it."

He was thinking about the first meeting with Kennedy, and the first meetings with all the bosses he had ever worked for. The love at first sight, like it is with a woman. The enthusiasm and the striving and the feeling that this is going to be the real thing. And then the gradual falling out of love, the slow melting of work into monotony into discontent and the desperate search for a new romance, always winding up one Saturday night with him in front of an empty desk and a full wastebasket, wondering if the next one was going to be any different.

He was thinking about a lot of things and, perhaps because he could hear her behind the partition and because so much of his life on the twentieth floor of this office building had been part of her life, and hers part of his, and it was all ending now, he kept thinking of Hilda.

He thought of Hilda with her slip always showing. He thought of the limp hair and the thick ankles and the shapeless lump of a body and the querulous voice and the myopic eyes peering hopefully through rimless glasses at a world that would always come into focus a little beyond her reach. And he wondered, as he had wondered so many times, whether being ugly on the outside was any worse than being like he was, and whether he too would some day discover a fantasy that helped. . . .

He recalled the first time she had complained to him about being forever annoyed by men. That one had been a man standing next to her on a crowded subway. Al had been with the firm only a few days, so he hadn't said anything. And then one rainy day when they had sent down for lunch and she had told him all about the fellow who kept calling her for a date, who claimed he'd noticed her in the elevator, Al had been on the verge of making a crack. But he had caught the look on her face, and something—he didn't know what it was—had kept him from doing it then, or ever after.

"It's awful the way men are," she always said, visiting at his desk when things got slow.

"Why, what happened?" Al would ask, as though he didn't know, approximately.

"Oh, last night I was at the movies and there was a man sitting next to me—a nice-looking man, too—and he started to work his arm around the back of my chair and before the picture was over he had his hand on my shoulder and he was talking to me and trying to make a date. The nerve."

And when she told it to a girl friend over the phone, the man had even kissed her.

Al had heard plenty from Hilda in five years, and so had others. He had heard about the man who followed her home from the subway one night and how she had had to call a cop. He had heard about the letters she was getting from a fellow on the ninth floor she hardly knew, letters so "awful" she threw them away (of course). He had heard about all the men who had bothered her on the beaches and street corners and trolleys and subways and busses and in the elevators and movie houses and by mail and telephone, and always it had been in the same outraged, indignant voice, and when he was unable to look her in the face as she told these things to him, he never knew whether it was because he was afraid of laughing or afraid of crying. . . .

Somewhere in another world an impatient cab driver was leaning on his horn, and at the other end of the hall a girl was laughing a Saturday night laugh, and a voice was calling to him.

"I'm going now, Al." It was Hilda. "Will you turn out the lights when you leave?"

He got up from the desk and stood in the doorway, watching her primping hopelessly before the mirror in the anteroom. Her whole body seemed to sag in weary, dispirited surrender to the glass.

She glanced at him. "You won't forget an old friend, will you? Be sure to phone us once in a while."

"Of course I will," he said, knowing that he'd never even see her again because she'd always be just a terribly homely girl whose heartbreak he had once known.

"I guess it's good-by, Al." She smiled her crooked little smile and opened the door.

He stepped across the room quickly. "Wait a minute." He took her hand and closed the door and pulled her close.

"Al," she said breathlessly. For a fleeting moment, her eyes searched his face eagerly, and then she drew back bewildered at what she saw there.

"Give us a kiss, honey, come on." He put a hand on her shoulder and his arm around her waist. "I've always wanted to—"

"Please, Al." She was backing into the corner, her face pale and frightened. "Al."

"Come on, Hilda. Stay here. You don't have to go yet. We're all alone." He grappled with her, and her handbag dropped to the floor. "One little kiss, come on."

"Leave . . . me . . . alone!" She tore at his chest and twisted in his arms, but he was too strong for her, and he had her backed into the corner and her head grasped tightly in his hands and he could feel her whole body recoil as he pressed his lips hard on hers.

"Don't!" she choked. With a sudden surge of desperation she broke away and snatched up her bag, but he was moving toward her again.

"Come here, baby."

"Don't touch me!" she screamed.

He caught her arm but she pulled away, and with all the strength left in her she lashed out and slapped him sharply in the face.

"You're just like the rest of them!" she cried harshly, her lips trembling. "You're all alike!"

With a little cry, she opened the door and ran out into the hall.

"Good-by, Hilda," he said softly to himself.

He could hear her hurrying down the corridor and then she was in the elevator, and he knew that by the time she reached the street her heart would have stopped pounding and the terrible hurt would already have started to heal.

He put on his hat and coat and took one long, last look at the office. Then he snapped off the lights and stepped out into the hall and watched the door slowly lock shut on part of his life, and somehow he didn't feel as bad as he had thought he would.

In a week or so, another man would be sitting at his desk. And when the work slowed down, or when Kennedy was gone for the day, or when it was raining out and there'd be luncheon sandwiches and coffee sent up from the drugstore, Hilda would be telling her stories to someone new. Only now, it would be different.

For her, at least, it would always be different.

You Can't Have Everything

She clung to my arm tightly, as though somehow that would show the others in the living room that *I* cared for *her*.

"Don't you want to dance?" she asked.

"I'm tired," I said.

"Is anything wrong, Roy?"

I turned to her, gazing at the plain, unbeautiful face that seemed to have been made for slapping. "I told you, Marsha," I said, "I'm tired. I've been working hard all week."

"Gee, I'm sorry, dear. I do want you to enjoy yourself. It's only for you that I have parties like this."

"For me? Why for me?" I demanded. "You know I don't go for these people."

She gave a little giggle. "I'm proud of you, silly. I like to have them look at you while I say to myself, 'He's mine. All mine.'"

I pulled my arm free.

"Roy—isn't that the way you feel when people look at *me?*"

I didn't answer.

"Roy?" Her eyes had me trapped.

"All this talk, honey," I said, looking away. "I'm worn out. It's Saturday night. Can't you let me relax?"

But she had already stopped listening. Sometimes not listening was the only protection she had. She drifted away to the kitchen, holding her quivering lips in a meaningless little smile, and I started breathing again. I stood there in the crowded, noisy room playing with my drink and wondering to myself, as I had wondered so many times in the past six months, how much longer I would be able to go on keeping Marsha Cornell dangling on the string while I played the field.

I glanced around the enormous room at the old masters on the walls, at the magnificent furnishings that had been brought over, piece by piece, from the finest establishments in Europe during the first hot flush of Mr. Cornell's newly attained affluence. The old guy had it all right—plenty of it—and a lot of it would be mine someday, just as soon as I popped the proper question. The only trouble was, it would be a package deal, and Marsha came in the package.

But what the hell—I shrugged and headed for the bar. . . . You can't have everything.

Halfway across the room I made the big mistake. I never should have turned my head. Because when I did, I saw the girl. She was on the powder-blue love seat beneath the Gainsborough. She had on a black, off-the-shoulder affair and she wasn't bothering to look even politely amused. I walked right over and sat down next to her.

"You mind?"

She turned cold gray eyes on me. "It's too early to tell." Then she smiled, and she was almost beautiful.

"Finish your drink," I said, "and I'll show you how to dance. Are you alone?"

"Practically. I came with Henry De Witt." She got rid of the glass. "He's out like a mazda in the guest room —on three drinks."

I laughed. "You sure pick 'em." Henry De Witt had gone straight from Harvard to a shiny desk at National City and his grandfather had left him a small fortune to play around with in his spare time, but he still was a terrible bust. He was too shy to talk and when he did talk no one liked what he said, and because he couldn't stand that, he'd pass out at parties as rapidly as the power of alcohol would permit. Everything he touched turned to lead. But this girl was definitely not lead. . . .

Someone had stacked oldies on the hi-fi and Tommy Dorsey was giving out with "You're a Sweetheart." We got up and she moved into my arms and we started a smooth slow-foxtrot and I knew right away that I wasn't going to show her how to dance. I wasn't going to show *her* anything.

"Tell me about you and Henry," I murmured to the scent of Jungle Gardenia in her hair.

"Must I?"

I thought it over for a moment. "No," I smiled, holding her a little closer. "By all means, no."

"What's your name?"

"Roy," I said. "Roy Samson."

"Oh . . ." She took her face from my shoulder and looked at me. You're . . . Marsha's . . ."

She winced as my hand dug into her back.

"Don't say that," I muttered harshly.

She hid her face. "I'm . . . I'm sorry. I must have confused you with—"

"You didn't confuse me with anyone. Just don't say it—that way."

We danced for a while, nursing the strained silence, until finally she asked, "What do you do, Roy?"

"I'm a junior customer's man at Harris, Upjohn and Company, down in the Street, if that means anything to you. I make a lot of money for some people and practically nothing for myself." And then, because I felt I had to, I added, "Marsha's father is my one big account."

"I see," she said simply, and I had an idea she did see.

"Now what about you?"

"Ursula Wynant," she said.

"Pretty."

"I model for—ha ha—a living." She kept talking, and I kept staring at her lips.

"Look," I broke in, "I don't suppose you'd care to do an off-to-Buffalo?"

She didn't answer for a long time. Then she said, "What about Marsha?"

"Let me do the worrying."

"And Henry?"

"Let him do the worrying." I eased her toward the foyer.

We got away without being too obvious. Marsha was still in the kitchen.

Outside, the cold night air was intoxicating. Or maybe it was the strange new hand held tightly in mine. We went to a small bar where the lights were kind, and we talked and drank and drank and talked, and occasionally the truth crept through the banter, and that was when the part that was the drinking suddenly seemed terribly necessary.

I kept staring at her pale, angular face, trying to decide what it was that made me feel she'd never do too well as a model, and it wasn't easy to figure out, because she wasn't far from being beautiful. She was a girl sitting at a bar in midtown Manhattan with a strange young man on a Saturday night and the future lay ahead, bright with promise and mystery. But as she talked, none of that seemed to mean as much to her as the dull years of poverty in a small Midwestern town that lay behind. And it was then, as she told me of the grubby jobs she had held before coming to New York, that I decided it was the eyes that were wrong, out of key with the rest of her. It was more than too much eye-shadow that gave them the faintly lurking sadness.

Suddenly the eyes made me uneasy. "Let's get out of here," I said.

We walked aimlessly for a couple of blocks, holding hands and not saying anything, and every now and then I could feel her looking at me, but I didn't mind the eyes in the darkness. I felt good walking at her side, better than I had felt in a long time, and I began to wonder what it would be like to feel that way for a lifetime . . . or at least a whole night, anyway.

Waiting at the curb for the light to change, I glanced at her and our eyes met and then I moved close and took her face in my hands.

"I don't know what the hell this is all about," I murmured, kissing her softly on the lips.

She didn't resist. "Don't you think we ought to be getting back to the party now?"

"Ursula, I want to be alone with you."

"Oh, Roy . . ." She shook her head and sighed a small, hopeless sigh.

"Please, honey."

We stood there at the curb and let the people stare at us. I didn't give a damn. I kissed her again. "Where do you live?" I said heavily.

"Well . . . I have a little place on Sixty-eighth just off Lexington. But . . . but the heat goes off at eleven. . . ."

"Shall we walk it?"

She gazed into my eyes until I had to look away. And then I heard her say, "It's later than you think, Roy."

And looking back on it now, I remember that I thought she meant the hour. We took a cab.

Her apartment was in one of those old private houses. It was small and poorly furnished. She hung up my hat and coat and brought drinks from the kitchenette.

"To us," I said. It wasn't Canadian Club and there were no canapés with it and the hooked rug beneath my feet wasn't wall-to-wall carpeting. But what the hell—you can't have everything.

"Don't go away," she said. "I'll be right back."

I didn't go away. Not then, I didn't.

But later, the blackness outside her windows started turning to gray and I was down to my last cigarette and I knew it was time to leave, but I wasn't sure just what it was I wanted to say.

"Ursula—honey—"

She covered my mouth quickly with her lips. "Don't, darling," she said. "Let's not talk about love."

I gazed at her for a moment. "Okay," I shrugged. "Okay by me."

When I came back from the closet with my hat and coat, her eyes searched mine anxiously. "But I *am* glad you sat down beside me tonight," she said. "Are you, Roy?"

I took her face in my hands. "What do you think?" It was late. I was tired. And she had said, "Let's not talk about love." So I said, "What do you think?"

It wasn't very clever.

Ma had roast beef for Sunday dinner, served with brown gravy and the usual questions: How was Marsha? Why did I stay out so late? How was Marsha? And how was Marsha?

"Please pass the potatoes, Pop."

"Why do you change the subject?" my mother asked.

"I'm not changing the subject. I happen to be rather hungry today."

"Marsha is a nice girl. She comes from a fine family. I don't know what you're waiting for."

"I'd rather not talk about it. Do you mind?" Not today I didn't want to talk about it. I wanted to go on remembering last night.

"How are you fixed for money these days?" my father said.

I glanced at him sharply. "Why do you ask?"

"Well, yesterday I got a bill from Tripler's for four hundred and twenty dollars for an overcoat, two suits and a dozen ties."

"Damn it!" I shouted, reddening. "I told them to send it to the office!"

"Roy!" my mother cried.

"I'll pay for it by the first of the month," I muttered to the plate.

"I wasn't worrying about that," my father said quietly. "I just wanted to know what it was all about. It seems to me that for a boy who is earning a hundred dollars a week, you have very expensive tastes. I hope you can afford them."

"Don't worry about it." I threw my napkin down and left the table.

I didn't want to have to tell them about the gin games with Mr. Cornell. At first, during the early weeks, I had gone around feeling good because I thought I was a guy who could play better gin than a man who smoked dollar cigars. I had even boasted about it a little. And then, slowly, I had become aware of the fact that he was throwing the games to me, and I knew then how very much the Cornells wanted me for Marsha, how high Mr. C. was prepared to go to keep me visiting their home and leaving contented. That gave me an even nicer feeling, cozy and secure . . . but it was nothing I cared to talk about.

So far, it had cost Mr. Cornell plenty. The latest figures on the cover of our score-sheet showed that he owed me twenty-three hundred dollars, and though neither of us had ever put it in so many words, we both knew under what happy circumstances payment in full would be made. . . .

I took a bus downtown and went window-shopping along the avenues, looking at the women and seeing only their mink coats, and looking at the Cadillacs and Lincolns and seeing only their price tags. It was then that I had to start thinking about Ursula Wynant again. But thinking about her didn't seem to be enough, so I went into a drugstore and dialed her number.

No answer.

I wasn't going to call Marsha Cornell. But I caught a glimpse of myself in the mirror behind the fountain and something that I saw there made me change my mind. It was one of the new suits from Tripler's. It looked damned good on me.

She answered on the third ring.

"Oh . . . Roy . . ." her voice wavered uncertainly.

"Are you angry, Marsha?"

She didn't say anything for a moment. "Why should I be angry?" I could almost see her pale lips trembling.

"About last night," I said. "About my leaving so early."

"You're—you're perfectly free—" she struggled with the words. "Free to do as you please."

"I was awfully tired, honey."

"I—I know. You told me several times. I—"

"What's the matter with your voice?"

"I have a cold," she blurted out. "Oh, Roy, couldn't you at least have said good night to me? Couldn't you—?"

"You were busy, honey, and I didn't want to start anything . . . with all those people there. You know how you get."

"No, Roy, I don't know. Tell me how I get."

"Well, you sort of . . . complain."

She gave a little moan. "Is that what I do? I complain. I must learn to stop, mustn't I . . ."

"Oh, it's not so bad."

"Thank you, Roy," she said weakly.

"Did Henry De Witt get home all right?" I made it sound casual.

"Two of the boys took him home. He's a sensitive boy.

That's why he has to drink so much . . . to deaden the pain. Liquor makes me sick. That's the only reason I don't touch it. She was so lovely, wasn't she?"

"Who?"

"Ursula Wynant. The girl Henry brought. . . ."

"Oh."

"The girl you left with."

I swallowed, groping for words. "Now, Marsha . . ."

"Do I sound complaining, Roy?" Her voice quivered. "I don't mean to."

"Look, honey, she asked me to drop her off on the way—"

"There's no need to explain."

"You know how a girl feels when she's left alone at a party."

"I do, Roy, don't I?" I could hardly hear her.

"Now if I wasn't all tied up tonight I'd come over and take you to a movie and in no time at all you'd get over any foolish notions about—"

"I don't feel well." Her voice broke. "I have to hang up now."

"Wait a minute, honey, you're not angry now, are you?"

"Good-by, Roy."

"I'll see you early in the week. Okay?"

"Will you?" It was a small moan. "Shall I wait at the telephone?"

"Now, Marsha. . . . Hello?"

But she had hung up. I stumbled from the booth, mopping my forehead. I was going to have to warm her up again the next time I saw her. I'd have to tell her I loved her. Maybe I'd even have to kiss her.

The trouble you could get into for only a dime . . .

Monday was a nightmare downtown. The tape was late from the opening and stocks were off one to five by noon. The boardroom was a madhouse and faces were long. But I was wearing a smile. I had put five hundred shares of Steel out on the short side for Mr. Cornell a few days before and now he was cleaning up, and the way I was smiling, you'd think it was my dough. You'd think it was mine already.

I phoned him after the close.

"See what I mean, Mr. Cornell? Four thousand dollars on a three-day trade. Not bad, not bad."

He grunted wordlessly.

I said, "You don't sound very excited."

"All right—four thousand dollars," he said in a flat voice. "It's only money."

"Only money. Hah! You bet it's only money."

"There are other things more important in life than money, Roy."

I had to laugh. *He* was the one to talk. "Like what, Mr. Cornell?"

Bitterness crept into his voice. "Like my daughter's happiness," he said. "But I don't have to tell *you* that, do I, Roy?"

"Of course not."

"I've told you many times that she's the only thing that means anything to me."

I was smiling to myself. I knew what he was getting around to.

"Certainly," I said.

"Are you doing anything tonight, Roy?"

"Why do you ask?" As though I didn't know.

"I thought . . . I thought maybe you'd come up and play a little gin."

"Gee, Mr. Cornell," I said, "I don't know if I'll be free tonight."

Worry him a little.

"You're busy these nights, Roy, aren't you?" There was a strange note in his voice.

"Not so very. It's just that—"

"How would you like it if we raise the stakes to fifty cents a point?"

"It's just that sometimes things come up unexpectedly and I'm never sure what I'm going to be doing, but I'll tell you what. I'll push everything aside and make it my business to see you tonight. How is Marsha feeling?"

"Say around eight-thirty, Roy?"

"Eight-thirty. Right." I grinned as I hung up. Fifty cents a point! I punched my open palm with my fist. Oh . . . brother!

The only trouble was, I'd have to put off seeing Ursula

until tomorrow. But what the hell—you can't have everything.

Downstairs, the streets were jammed with people rushing for subways, people like myself who couldn't wait to get away from the places in which they spent most of their waking lives. The difference between them and me was: someday soon, I'd get away for good.

I saw him standing there on the sidewalk in front of the entrance, but I didn't duck away fast enough. Henry De Witt caught up with me.

"Hello, Roy," he said in that soft, weary voice of his. "I knew if I waited, I'd find you."

"What's up, Henry?" I kept moving in the direction of Broad.

He cleared his throat as he fell in step with me. "It's —it's about Ursula. You know . . . the girl at the party."

"What about her?" I walked faster.

"Well, nothing really." He hesitated. "I just wanted to . . . that is, Marsha told me you . . . Well, I mean, thanks for being such a good sport."

"Forget it."

"It was awfully decent of you to come through for me in a pinch and take her home the way you did."

"I said forget it!" I felt like slugging him.

"She wasn't angry with me, was she?" His eyes blinked with anxiety.

I stared at the pale face. "Why? Haven't you spoken to her?"

"I . . . I'm afraid to call." He grinned sheepishly. "I thought I'd give her time to cool off first."

I had to laugh to myself. I was never going to let her cool off.

"No," I said, "she wasn't angry."

He sighed gratefully. "You've got to let me buy you a drink."

I shrugged. "If you insist."

We went into Schuyler's and stood at the bar. The martini felt good going down, but I had to listen to Henry with it. He was gabbing about Ursula, stammering out the details of his first date with her, and I tried not to hear him but he kept moving closer. Then he lowered his voice confidentially.

"You can keep a secret, can't you?"

I looked at my watch, bored. "Anytime . . . anyplace."

"She didn't . . . I mean . . ." He lowered his eyes in confusion. "Ursula didn't tell you, did she?"

"Tell me what?" I picked idly at the olive in my glass.

"That . . . well, about our getting married next week."

The bartender jumped forward with the rag. "Oops! Here, let me get you another."

"No," I said hoarsely, "that's all right."

He wiped up the drink. "Don't be silly. It'll only take—"

"I said no!" I turned. "I've got to run, Henry."

"Wait a minute," Henry said, "I haven't even—"

"I'm getting out of here." I moved for the door and he ran after me.

"You'll keep it under your hat, won't you?" He held my arm.

"Let go, will you?"

He followed me to the sidewalk, talking fast. "She doesn't wear the ring at parties. It's a week from Saturday. No ceremony. Mother doesn't know yet. She wouldn't approve, so we're not going to tell her until it's too late for her to do anything about it. You won't say anything?" He clung to me. "Roy . . .?"

"Don't worry," I snapped, brushing him aside. "Now will you lay off? I have to get uptown."

But fast. Suddenly I felt as though I'd stop breathing if I didn't see her right away, laugh about all this right away . . .

He said, "Can I give you a ride in my car?"

I turned to him with a sick look. "Your . . . car?"

"Yes. I just got it. A Caddy. Come on, it's just up the block."

"No," I said quickly. "No, thanks." And I fled up the street. A great kidder, that Henry. *He* was going to marry Ursula Wynant a week from Saturday. Ha!

Uptown, I ran the two blocks from the subway station. I pushed her bell and banged on the door for five minutes, but it was no use. She wasn't home.

There was a restaurant on the corner, and because it was dinnertime, I went in and ordered a meal, but all I could do was stare at the food and watch the clock. It was almost eight o'clock when I returned.

The light was on in her window and my heart leaped. "Who is it?" I heard her voice, muffled behind the closed door.

"Roy," I sang out.

"Who?"

"Roy Samson." Was she kidding?

The door swung open and I choked up at the sight of her loveliness.

"Hello," I said airily. "May I?"

"This *is* a surprise." She wasn't smiling. "Come in."

The living room wasn't quite the way I had remembered it. Somehow, it seemed just a little smaller and a little plainer. I threw my hat and coat on the sofa and took her hands in mine.

"Ursula, honey." I examined her face. Then I kissed it. Her lips were cold. "Baby," I said, "how I've missed you. It's been almost two whole days."

She looked at me uncertainly. "Would you like a drink?"

"Yes," I said. "I sure would." All at once I needed one desperately. The coldness of her lips . . . the look on her face . . .

She came back and I took the glass eagerly. "I called you so many times yesterday," I said.

She nodded. "I know."

"You know?"

"I heard the phone ringing."

I set the glass down. "But, honey, why didn't you answer?"

"Because—" She averted her eyes. "Because I knew it would be you."

I stepped to her quickly and took her arm. "Ursula, look at me."

"Please, Roy." She pulled away.

But I wouldn't let go. "Honey," I said softly. I drew her to me and held my lips to hers, feeling her stiffen, then relax in my arms. "Why didn't you want it to be me?"

She didn't answer.

My voice rose to a shout. "Why didn't you want it to be me?"

She broke away and went to the window. "Please go, Roy. Please. I don't . . . I don't want . . ."

"You don't want what?" I cried out.

She turned and I saw the anguish on her face. "I don't want to fall in love with you!"

The words hit me in the pit of my stomach—*I don't want to fall in love with you*—and all I could do was stand there dumbly as the truth crept over me like a sickness, knowing all at once that that was what I had wanted, really, more than anything else in the world.

"Jesus, honey," I groaned, "but what about—what about the other night?"

"It was wonderful . . . a treasure . . ." I heard her voice. Her face was turned to the window again. "I'll always remember it. Don't spoil it, Roy."

And the bitterness was upon me. "He was right, then," I sneered. "He wasn't kidding." I grabbed the glass from the table.

She turned. "Who?"

"I saw Henry this afternoon." I drained the glass. "He told me everything. You are to be congratulated." My face twisted. "Congratulations. Here comes the bride—all dressed in a Cadillac."

She came over to me. "Please, please don't be angry."

"I'm not angry," I snapped, shoving her hand away. "What have I got to be angry about? I hardly know you. I've got no claims. You said it yourself, didn't you? Let's not talk about love, that's what you said. Okay. Let's not talk about love." I moved for my hat and coat. "Let's not talk about anything. Let's especially not talk about Henry De Witt."

"Roy—wait a minute!" She held on to my arm, and something in her voice cried out to me.

"All right." My lips trembled. "I'm waiting."

She buried her face on my chest, and I knew then that she was crying. "I'm so sorry, Roy, but please try to forgive me. I guess I was hoping you'd be as casual as most men are. Maybe I was selfish, but when you feel you're going under the waves for the last time you want to take one last look around at all that you'll never have again. . . ."

"What do you mean?" I pulled her face up angrily. "Why never again? Why does it have to be a lifetime with Henry De Witt? Why?"

"Look at me," she pleaded. "Can't you see it written all over my face? Look around at this shabby apartment. Can't you understand how it can be that there are too many things I want too much because I never had them at all? They're the things that money can buy, Roy—not love—and I can't help myself any more for wanting them. Didn't you ever want the things that money can buy?"

"What's that got to do with it?" I cried out in sudden fury. . . . "Never mind what *I* want!" . . . Knowing that my anger had betrayed me.

She regarded me for a moment. "We're so much alike, aren't we? We'd never have been right for each other anyway. We need the Henrys . . . and the Marshas . . ."

"Marsha?" I grabbed her wrist. "What's she got to do with this?"

"They're always there waiting for us," Ursula went on. "The submissive, who have to buy what they want, waiting for the dominant to come along and swallow them up. It's something like your Stock Exchange, Roy. Always sell in a rising market, before you get too old or too unattractive to find a buyer."

"No," I cried, turning away. "It's not true." The words sounded hollow to my ears. "That isn't the way it is."

"It is for me, Roy," she said quietly.

"No." I shook my head weakly, trying not to see the clock on the bookcase, silent reminder of a waiting card table, a hopeful father and a girl who wanted me to gaze into her wounded eyes for the rest of our natural lives.

"I know what I want out of life," Ursula was saying, "and I'm not going to trade it in for love."

"Honey, please!" I took her in my arms.

"It's no use." She struggled. "I could love you . . . much too easily, Roy. But it's too late."

"You've got to listen to me!" I pleaded with her, holding her close and seeking her lips as though to still her protests, knowing that I wasn't really fighting for her —I was fighting for myself. "Listen to me now!" I shouted.

"No!" She broke away with a desperate cry and ran to the door. "Oh God, please get out, Roy!"

"Honey—"

"Get out!" She tore open the door and stood there tensely. "Can't you see?" she implored. "It's got to be good-by."

I stared at her. I watched her until the crumbling face was no longer beautiful, and a sneer managed to find its way to my lips. She was just another girl, that was all . . . a girl who couldn't stop knowing what she wanted out of life long enough to give me a reprieve . . . a stay of execution.

"Okay, baby," I said quietly. "Anything you say." I went past her and took up my hat and coat.

"You're not angry, Roy?" Her voice reached out to me hopefully.

"Angry? No." I smiled a crooked little smile. "Just bored."

"Roy—"

I sauntered out without even looking back.

What the hell . . . you can't have everything. Maybe it was time I stopped trying. I glanced at my watch. I was late. The old man would be fretting and Marsha would be sitting there on the sofa biting her stubby fingernails. Maybe it was time to get down on one knee, mouth a few pretty words and begin to cash in on a lifetime of ease. The field was getting dull, anyway.

"The field is for suckers," I said to myself in the darkness of the cab. I stopped off on the way and bought a box of candy.

And then I was strolling through the lobby, past the gold-braided doorman and the plush, unused furniture and the picture windows that looked out upon useless, well-manicured gardens. I caught sight of myself in the mirror-lined walls of the elevator, and I saw that my face was pale and thin. I had been trying too hard. The rest would do me good. A nice long lifetime of rest. . . .

Mr. Cornell answered the door.

"I'm late," I said, breezing past him into the foyer.

He shuffled the unlit cigar to the other side of his mouth. "Give me your hat and coat, Roy."

"Candy, too." I put the package on the sideboard. "Sweets for the sweet. And where *is* my little sweetie?"

I went into the living room, drinking in the soft, rich glow of its dimly lighted splendor. It was a beautiful room, the kind of room that made you wonder what you could have been seeking in the tawdry flats of the Ursula Wynants. This was it. This was what I wanted and this was what I was going to have.

I sang out, "Marsha?" waiting for the archway to spew her into my arms.

Mr. Cornell came in. "Have a drink, Roy?"

"No, thanks," I said. "Where's everybody?"

"Mrs. Cornell is in her bedroom. She doesn't feel well."

"I'm sorry to hear that." I sank comfortably into a club chair. "You want to tell Marsha I'm here? Tell my little—"

"Marsha is out."

I looked up at him, blinking. "Marsha? Out?" I laughed.

"She is out . . . with a young man. . . ." He picked the words carefully. "Out for the evening . . . on a date . . . with a boy from my office . . . who . . . who is very much interested in her."

I chuckled. "Really?"

"Is there a joke, Roy?" His lips began to quiver. "Is it so strange and humorous that men should be interested in a lovely   charming young creature . . ." He sounded as though he were going to cry. "A sweet . . . intelligent girl who . . . who . . ."

I got up from the chair and went right past him. I went down the long hallway straight to her bedroom and tried the door. It was locked.

"Marsha?" I rattled the knob.

I heard the muffled sob on the other side.

"Honey," I called out, "come on now—stop acting foolish."

No answer.

"Marsha!" I shouted, pounding on the door. "Do you hear me?"

I went back to the living room, to the old man. "What's this all about?" I demanded.

He looked at me with haggard eyes. "My daughter is out for the evening," he said in a proud, hollow voice. "She is out on a date. . . ."

"Yeah, yeah."

"She asked me to give you a message." He seemed to straighten up as he spoke. "She doesn't care to have you call her any more. She doesn't want to see you. That was what she told me to tell you before she went out with the boy from my office."

I licked my dry lips. "We'll see about that." I started for the foyer.

He came after me. "Wait a minute—"

I stopped and looked down at his hand on my arm. A smile came to my face. "You didn't let me get very far, did you?"

"Where are you going, Roy?" he asked quietly.

"You said she was out."

"That's right." He began to lead me back. "But you came to see *me*, remember? We're going to play a little gin rummy tonight. No?"

He led me across the living-room carpet.

"Fifty cents a point, Roy."

"But, Mr. Cornell—"

"Isn't that what we agreed?" His grip tightened.

I nodded dumbly. "Yes, but—"

"All right, then." He opened the library door. The card table was all set up, waiting for me. "Take off your jacket, Roy. Make yourself comfortable."

He sat down at the table and began to shuffle the cards with swift, practiced skill.

I stood there, feeling my hands growing cold.

"Mr. Cornell—" I began in a feeble voice.

He was gazing at the score sheet. "Twenty-three hundred dollars," he said softly. "And all I ever wanted for her was happiness."

"Mr. Cornell—can't we—?" I swallowed.

"Sit down, Roy." He brought a flame to his cigar.

"Can't we talk this over?"

He looked up at me.

"Sit down," he said, "and cut the cards."

He Brung Happiness to Millions

Yep. Know whatcha mean. Seems like a long ride but ackshelly it's nearer Mr. Hackett's place this way than if I would of met your train at L.A. what with that downtown traffic, oh brother. So jus' relax. Sit back and enjoy the scenery. You already come three thousand miles, this is oney a drop in the bucket and you're there. This your first trip out here, Mr. Talbot? . . .

I thought so. Knew I never seen you at Mr. Hackett's or at the broadcast. Welp, all I can say is, you're gonna like it out here. This is God's country and Mr. Hackett is a fine man. Fourteen years now I been with him and ain't got a cause for complain. Except maybe those jokes he tells about me on the air, about Willy the chauffeur, that's me natchelly, but hell, I don' really mind. It's jus' my missus nags me I oughta get paid extra if he's gonna make fun of me and call me a punchy stumble-bum over the television. She didn' even want me to sign no release, you know how women are. You ain't married, are you? . . .

Di'n' think so. I can always tell. Suppose you're the new gag writer for the program, huh? . . .

Uh oh. Strike one against Willy. Not that you sound like no gag writer, don' get me wrong, Mr. Talbot. It's jus' that there's usually quite a few of 'em comin' and goin' and as a matter of fac' oney las' week when I'm drivin' Lenny Stack to the station and tellin' him how sorry I am the boss don' renew his contract he says to me: "Don' worry, Willy" he says. "There'll be another

109

one jus' like me before long." So you see I figure you
was it, 'cause you're a young, good-lookin' guy like
Lenny Stack (you're welcome) and you look like a writer
too. I could of sworn—

A *what?* . . .

Ha ha. You're a mighty healthy-lookin' ghost there,
Mr. Talbot. Yes, sir. Stop me if I ast too many questions.
The boss always says I ast too many questions. But jus'
exackly what is the ghost gonna ghostwrite? Ha ha . . .

Ya don' say? An autobiography book. The Life of
Monty Hackett. That's grand. Wonnerful. You're gonna
have a mighty fine book there, Mr. Talbot, and you
wanna know somethin'? It'll make a mighty fine movin'
pitcher too, and that sure would make the boss happy
'cause I know how much he wants his life story in
pitchers, ever since that Al Jolson pitcher ten, twelve
years ago. Mr. Hackett seen the Jolson pitcher three
times and I hear him tell Manny Zack, that's his agent,
I hear him tell Manny that Jolson's life's not half
as inarresting and inspirational as the life of Monty
Hackett, but of course he's too modest to come right
out and do somethin' about it. And believe me it's about
time they *done* a pitcher about Mr. Hackett's life. Ain't
he a great name in show business for years and ain't he
a fine, outstandin' example of a good man? Look at all
them charities he works for and what a fine family man
he is and how he keeps sendin' food and clothes to his
folks in the old country *every* Christmas and how good
he is to Clarabelle. . . .

Her? Oh, that's Mr. Hackett's daughter. Don' you
remember those skits and jokes he used to do on the program about Clarabelle? Years ago on the old radio show,
before TV. Jeez, they was funny, about poor Monty
Hackett bein' stuck with a homely daughter and how
dumb she was and how was he ever gonna to get rid of
her, funniest damn thing on the program. He used to
have a special writer who done nothin' but the Clarabelle stuff, Frankie Rool, helluva guy, wonder whatever
happen to Frankie? But Mr. Hackett don' do the Clarabelle gags no more. Y'know, the public they get tired
hearin' the same stuff over and over. And when the kid
come home from the sanitarium—

Yeah, someplace out in Westwood. She took all them aspirin tablets outta the bottle at one time or somethin'. I dunno, they called it a nervous breakdown but it wasn't nothin' as bad as all that. Jus' overwork, I guess. The kid knock herself out with the schoolwork, always sittin' home up in her room bonin' over the books, stayin' away from people, never out playin' and partyin' like the other girls, and her with all the advantages of bein' a celebrity. In fac', what with those jokes about her on the air every week, you could even say she was famous. But that was way back, and now that she's growed up— must be about your age, I'd say—Mr. Hackett is still the fine father he always was, nothin' too good for Clarabelle, nothin' he wouldn' do for her. So you see if you need any help on this here autobi—on this here book, why you jus' come to Willy and ast me anythin' you want, anythin' at all. I been with Mr. Hackett fourteen years and there's plenty that maybe he forgot or don' wanna tell you 'cause he's jus' natchelly a modest man. It's the writers that keep puttin' in all that stuff on the program about how much money he raises for all them charities. He don' wanna talk about nothin' he does. . . .

Like what? Well like, for instance, as I was sayin', the way he sends things to his old man and old lady in Europe, and does he go braggin' about it? Nah. Not like some people. Why you wouldn' even know he *got* folks over there, not from Mr. Hackett you wouldn'. Betcha hardly nobody even know it. And when the old folks ast to be sent for to come over here, the boss don' care how much it hurts him when he writes them to stay where they are and where they'll be happy amongst their own people and they can speak the language. No sir, Mr. Talbot, you don' find many sons like that, what thinks oney about what's best for others.

Oh-oh, here comes that drizzle again. But don' worry, it don' last long out here. God's country. And wait'll you see the room you're gettin'. I never seen it myself, but Gussie—that's my wife—Gussie tell me all about it. She was fixin' it up and gettin' it ready for you soon as Lenny Stack check out. Not that Mr. Hackett is runnin' no *hotel* up there in Bel-Air, but jeez, the way they come and go, sometimes you wonder. First Fred Wurlitzer, the announcer, and then Les Gibbons, you know, the vocalist, and then Arthur Crewes and then Mel Simmons and then all them writers, one after another, Lenny Stack the last of them, all of 'em nice young guys like you. And I'm telling you, the way Mr. Hackett extend the hospitality of the house to each and every one of them, why it's wonnerful. And I sure hope you ain't one of them ungrateful kind, like some of them, if you'll pardon the expression, Mr. Talbot. . . .

Whadda I mean ungrateful? This is what I mean ungrateful. The boss sends for a guy from New York, like you, and gives him a swell job on the show and as if that ain't enough to make him happy, does he make him check into a hotel and pay rent and live all alone in a strange city? Nah. Not Monty Hackett. *He* invites him into his home and lets him live there, for nothin', mind you, and wait'll you see the room, overlookin' the swimmin' pool, and not only that. He knows young guys like you and Les Gibbons and Lenny Stack are kinda lonely when you first come out here so he invites you to dinner with Mrs. Hackett and Clarabelle, jus' like it's your own home, and he knows you don' know nobody right off so he lets you take Clarabelle out at night to Ciro's and Mocambo and all them places and it's on *his* cuff, 'cause that's the kinda guy the boss is, and if you got any spare time over the weekends you don' have to worry that you got no girl to keep you company 'cause he's nice about his daughter. Mr. Hackett ain't no snob, no sirree. He's strickly an old-fashioned guy at heart, jus' like on the program. Why, when he hear about Jerry Loomis, you remember him, he was the crooner on the show las' fall, when he hear that Jerry gonna marry that girl from New York, Mr. Hackett fire him right away, for his own good. Sure. Even though he need Jerry badly on the program, the best low-price crooner in the business, but that's the kinda man Mr. Hackett is, more worried that a marriage should work out right. A husband belongs where his wife is, that's what he says to Jerry, and when Jerry move outta the house and head back for New York, does he tell everyone what a fine man Mr. Hackett is and how fine he been treated out here? Nah. That's what I mean ungrateful. And I ain't even gonna *tell* you the kinda things he spreads about the boss, they ain't worth repeatin', and Mrs. Hackett don' believe a word of it anyway. And this Les Gibbons, the tenor, who moves in after Loomis leaves, he ain't much better. Four weeks and he quits. The climate, he says. Hoddaya like that? The climate's too damp for his sinus. After Mr. Hackett goes to all the trouble to have new wallpaper put in the room and calls Clarabelle home from Palm Springs jus' so's this Gibbons don' feel like he's all alone out here. I ask you. . . .

Yeah, that's right, this is Hollywood now. Cantcha tell? The air smells different. God's country. Up ahead's the Strip. You hearda Sunset Strip. I'll show you where that Winston dame took the shot at Mr. Hackett. I guess that was before your time. . . .

No, she di'n' hit him. Drunk as a lord, lucky she di'n' hurt no one. None the less, they give her five years. . . .

Hodda *I* know why? Crazy, I guess. Or like I was sayin', ungrateful. Mr. Hackett di'n' have to be payin' her all that money every month like he was doin', but he was sorry for her after her husband knock himself off. . . .

I don' know. 'Cause he was broke, I guess. One of them tired TV actors, always outta work, always makin' excuses. Used to go around imaginin' the reason he couldn' get no job was 'cause the boss had him blackballed around the networks for bein' fresh to him. Strickly a no-talent crackpot. And when he hang himself, Mr. Hackett lets bygones be bygones and helps the widow out every month for I don' know how many years, and what does she do? Tries to kill him. Oh brother. It mus' be the climate. There's the spot now, see? On your left, we're jus' passin' it. Used to be a night club. Guess you'll be puttin' all that in your book, huh? Oughta make a inarresting scene in a pitcher. You know, the more you think about the boss, the more you see what a story you got there, Mr. Talbot. And I been thinkin', maybe The Life of Monty Hackett ain't such a hot title after all. You gotta get somethin' more to the point, like . . . like . . . yeah, how about callin' it: He Brung Happiness to Millions? Hey, that ain't bad if I say so myself. Jus' ast me anythin'. Willy the writer, ha ha. He Brung Happiness to Millions. Not bad at all. Say, I hope I'm not drivin' too fast for you, Mr. Talbot? After I leave you off at the house I gotta make time over to Beverly Hills and pick Clarabelle up at the head doctor and then I gotta hustle her over to the beauty parlor, and if I don' get her back home in time to have lunch with you the boss chews my hide off somethin' fierce. Betcha can't wait to get there, huh, Mr. Talbot? . . .

The Small Sound of Applause

Rob Kiplinger was tired . . . tired of the morning fogs and tired of the afternoon sunshine . . . tired of the good pictures he never produced, tired of all the money it made for him . . . tired of the people who loved him, baby . . . above all tired of being Rob Kiplinger and of the knowledge that no matter how tired he was of being Rob Kiplinger he would probably never make the slightest effort to be something better.

He sat at his massive desk, gloomily examined the sprawling litter of unfinished business, noted that it was twenty past five of a dying October afternoon, and scowled impatiently as his secretary padded in noiselessly over the thick beige carpeting.

"I'm sorry, Mr. Kiplinger," she announced.

"I'm sorry, too, Miss Delmar," he said, looking out of the French windows at the California sun trying to make believe that it wasn't autumn. "I'm sorry I ever left New York. I'm sorry my brother-in-law knew the head of this studio. I'm sorry my name isn't Darryl F. Zanuck. I'm sorry I have been given a secretary who is always walking in here and being sorry about something. What is it you're sorry about this time?"

"I'm sorry, Mr. Kiplinger," said Miss Delmar, "but that girl is here. The one that called twice this morning. She said Ferdinand Saxon told her to see you about—"

"Yes," Kiplinger said flatly, letting Miss Delmar wait while he squeezed the sweet nectar from a tiny delay of the inevitable. Then he looked up and said, "What was her name again?"

"Janice Barker. She got in from New York yesterday."

"Okay," he sighed, and Miss Delmar padded out again. His fingers moved automatically to the knot of his tie, but there was no tie. He had been in Hollywood for five years, but somehow his hands had never learned to accept the fact that the rightful place of his tie had been usurped by a paisley scarf, a pretender to the throne. He made an effort to pull the loose ends of his nerves together into what he hoped was a semblance of the kind of man who had good digestion and who would think Miltown was the name of a horse. Then he called jovially, "Come in—Come in!"

The girl walked in a little too casually to be genuinely casual, and Kiplinger's quick, practiced eyes photographed her from head to toe in a rapid-shutter exposure. She would be even more beautiful if she were smiling. Why couldn't they ever get it into their heads that it isn't attractive to look scared? Unless you're playing opposite the creature from the black lagoon.

"*Hel*-lo," he cooed. He stood up and took her proffered hand and held it between his large, warm hands, and he noticed that hers was cold and that her blue eyes were not smiling with her mouth. "Sit down, honey," he said. "How was the trip? Tell me about Ferdie Saxon. Tell me about yourself. Tell me about everything."

"The trip was simply horrid," she said, sinking into the green club chair. She recited the details and Kiplinger shook his head sympathetically, though he was only half listening. She had fine, small features and long auburn hair and good legs and there were no circles under her eyes and to Kiplinger her beauty was exquisite, but he was struck with the vague feeling that whatever she had was not for films and could be put to better use making some young man happy, or miserable, for the rest of his life.

"Didn't Mr. Saxon write to you about me?" she was saying. "He promised me he would before I left."

"Well, you know how it is," he said. "Our mailing room probably sent the letter to the story department by mistake, where it was quickly synopsized by a reader, bought by the studio, scripted by a former Theatre Guild playwright, and is probably being shot this very minute on Sound Stage Three, right over there." He pointed out of the open French windows, but when he saw the disappointment clouding her face, he added, "No, honey, I'm sorry. I received no letter about you from Ferdie. But why let that bother you? You're here. I'm here. I love you."

"Mr. Kiplinger," the girl said, a little too desperately, he thought, "I do want so terribly to get into pictures. Mr. Saxon said you would help me, and it means so awfully much to me."

He tapped the desk nervously with a pencil.

"I've had quite a bit of acting experience, Mr. Kiplinger: Lots of television, and two seasons at the Cape Playhouse in Dennis. Of course, that's only summer stock, but Mr. Aldrich told someone he thought I had a charming stage personality, and last spring I had a small part in *Louder and Funnier*. It died in Boston, but the critic on the *Herald* was awfully nice to me. Mr. Saxon says that's where he saw me. . . ."

"Tell me something," Kiplinger said, scowling, "are you a . . . a personal friend of Ferdie Saxon?"

"Well . . . frankly, no . . . not really," she apologized, looking down at her hands and not seeing his scowl relax. "I met him at one of those cocktail parties at the St. Regis, for Fred Gimble, the movie director. I spilled some Scotch on my dress, and Ferdie Saxon came over and helped me clean it, and naturally we got to talking. When I happened to tell him that I was going to the Coast soon and that I would do anything, but really *anything*, to get into pictures, he laughed and said, 'Well, then—why don't you see Rob Kiplinger?' Everyone there laughed—for the life of me I couldn't see why—but they all agreed with him."

He cleared his throat sharply and threw the pencil down on the desk, but the trouble with clearing your throat is that you clear only your throat, and getting rid of a pencil is just as futile because you don't get rid of anything but the pencil.

"He really thinks the world of you, Mr. Kiplinger. They all do."

"Yes, I know," he muttered, thinking of the admiration he had once hoped for and comparing the dream with the reality. "They all do."

"Every time your name came up Mr. Gimble said, 'That Kiplinger, quite a guy!' or something like that. I guess I shouldn't be telling you this, Mr. Kiplinger, but I always say that flattery isn't worth a darn if the person being flattered doesn't know about it. Don't you agree?"

He nodded, because nodding was easier than saying something like, "Insinuation is the sincerest form of flattery," and watching the blank look that would come to her face.

"Oh, yes," she went on, "I almost forgot *the* most important thing of all: Mr. Saxon told me to be sure to ask you to do a sketch of me. He told me all about your career as a scenic designer and how you studied art in Paris when you were a boy and how you once had an exhibit at the Museum of Modern Art and still loved to do sketches of your friends even though your work here in Hollywood no longer had anything to do with art. And he made me repeat one sentence over and over so I wouldn't forget it when I got here: 'Ferdie Saxon says he thinks I would make a wonderful subject for you.' That was it."

Kiplinger heard the chuckle—Miss Delmar's chuckle. He had heard it so many times before. It was not a chuckle of mirth or derision. Rather it was a chuckle of admiration and respect, a small pat of applause for a reputation that was transcontinental and that perpetually enhanced itself, like a self-winding clock.

"I certainly do agree with them. You're a perfect subject," he said, a little more loudly than was necessary, for Miss Delmar's desk was only a few feet off the entrance to his private sanctum. "And just to show you that I mean what I say, I'm going to do your portrait for you this very evening. That is, unless you're busy and—"

"No, not at all, I'd love to," she said eagerly.

"All right then, just as soon as we've had a bite to eat we'll go over to my hotel. . . ."

"Your hotel?"

"I know. I know. You don't understand why I'm living in a hotel instead of in a palace in Beverly Hills, but, honey, the servant problem is not just something we thought up as a good topic for bad films. The light here in my office happens to be very poor, so I keep all my drawing equipment over at my hotel."

"I . . . see," the girl said very slowly, and he knew that at last she did see. "Well, really, I don't think I ought to put you to all that bother, Mr. Kiplinger, and to tell you the truth—"

"Unh, unh, remember now, honey, you're in Hollywood. Absolutely no telling of the truth permitted. So not another word. It's settled."

He was not looking directly at her. He did not want to see frightened blue eyes. He was looking out through the entrance to his office, across the anteroom, to the glass panes of the modernistic bookcase against the wall. Miss Delmar was at her observation post. He hadn't doubted that for a moment. From her desk, she could watch the bookcase and see a reflection of everything that went on in his office. It gave her a visual movie to go with the sound track. It was vital that Miss Delmar enjoy the movies he put on for her.

"I think I'd like to do you in water colors," he said. "I hardly think crayon or charcoal would do justice to your lovely hair or to those eyes."

She blushed, and he wondered if Miss Delmar's movie was in Technicolor, and for a moment he thought of all the sketches he had done in the years since he had left the work he loved because he had feared being a failure at it, to wind up eventually as a producer of inferior motion pictures. Dozens of bad films and dozens of sketches, and it was the sketches that had counted.

A few of them hung in the foyer of his suite at the hotel. But most of them had been given to their subjects and thus put back in circulation where they could do the most good for their creator—the framed *fait accompli*, the diploma on the wall, the testimonial not to the art of Rob Kiplinger but to the genius that made him, or rather allowed him to be, what he was. That Kiplinger. What a guy. His motion pictures stink but did you hear about the time he . . .

He held out his hands and said, "Come here."

She got up and walked around the huge desk to his chair and he took both her hands and drew her toward him. He looked toward the bookcase for a moment and then he said, "You're a damned lovely kid, do you know it? Come here." He drew her head down and kissed her quickly on the lips. "Sit down over there and listen to me do something nice for you."

She did not say anything, but by the time she had reached the sofa, he could see that she had managed to bring back a smile to her face, and she said, with too much composure, "You're a dear, Mr. Kiplinger."

He called Miss Delmar in. The chuckle was now the trace of a smile. "I'm sorry, Mr. Kiplinger," she said, "but did you call me?"

"Get me Spindell on the phone," he said, "and on the way out would you be good enough to close the door?" He had let her see enough of this particular picture. A scene or two was always sufficient. It was wonderful how you could always count on people without any imagination to do a lot of imagining. As soon as he left, she would call Harry Lyons' secretary, and Lyons' secretary would call that idiot over at Paramount, and on it would go until it became a feature-length film . . . perhaps, by the time it got back to him wrapped up neatly in applause, a double feature. That Kiplinger. I'm . . . telling . . . you.

The extension rang and he picked up the phone. "Max? Rob Kiplinger. . . . Swell, tootsie, swell. . . . Max, I . . . No, I mean it, Max, I don't usually go overboard for farce comedy but this time . . . Yes, Max, a very lovely job. . . . Max, I have a girl sitting here next to me, name is Janice Barker . . . That's right. . . . You haven't, huh? Well, then you haven't been reading the papers, tootsie, and you haven't been watching that TV screen like you should. She's been all over the place, and not just good, but *great,* and why should I tell you how beautiful she is when you'll see that for yourself? . . . Just what you've been looking for, Max. . . . Of course I've seen her. . . . Sure. . . . I caught her in a show last year in Boston when I was . . . What? . . . (What was the name of that show, honey?) . . ."

"*Louder and Funnier,*" she said eagerly.

"*Louder and Funnier,* Max. . . . That's right. . . . My idea was, give her a stock contract to start, put her through the works and let her carry the ball from there.

. . . What? . . . Well, what do *you* think? You oughta know better than to ask that. . . . Sure . . . in water colors, too. . . . Uh huh. . . . Swell, that's fine. . . . (Take this down, honey.) . . . Ten o'clock tomorrow morning. . . . Through Gate 3. . . . Ask for Miss Trueman. . . . Max, I love you. . . . Thank you, baby."

"Oh, Mr. Kiplinger," the girl squealed when he had hung up. "Ferdie Saxon was right. You *are* wonderful!"

"You don't have to worry about a thing now, honey," he said, without smiling. "Just look pretty, don't speak unless you're spoken to, keep your ears open till you find out who's important and who's just acting important, and you're in. And if you don't follow my advice, that won't matter either, because Max Spindell doesn't know how to say 'no' to me."

She laughed a little hysterically and said, "I know this sounds silly, but really how can I ever thank you?"

The door was closed, so Kiplinger just looked at her and said, "The first thing you can do is drag me out of this office."

They stepped out into the anteroom.

"I'm leaving now," he said to Miss Delmar, who tried, with little success, to take her eyes off the girl. "I had a tentative engagement with Lester Stiles for dinner tonight. If he calls, tell him how sorry I am that I can't make it. I'll be at the hotel all evening if he wants to call me. But only if it's urgent. I'll leave that to you, Miss Delmar."

He took the girl's arm as they walked out, and he could hear Miss Delmar dialing her phone before he was halfway down the corridor to the elevator, and without ever having heard her personal calls he was certain he knew what she'd be saying, for a producer can be a hero to his own secretary if he's the wrong kind of man and she's the right kind of secretary.

"Mr. Kiplinger," the girl was saying, "I really don't want you to break your dinner date and go to all this trouble just for me. Honestly."

"Don't talk nonsense," was all he said, though what he might have said was, don't talk nonsense, I had no date with Lester Stiles. . . . I haven't spoken to him in four weeks, and he is, this very minute, three thousand

miles from here, in all probability having dinner at
Lindy's. . . .

Outside, the early evening air was toying with the idea
of fireplaces and extra blankets, and Kiplinger stood with
the girl for a moment before the entrance to the sprawling white building until Harry Davis, who drove one of
the studio limousines, spotted them and pulled up to the
curb. Harry had once been a studio stunt man and had
gone over a cliff on a motorcycle once too often. And so
now he clung to the payroll as semiprivate chauffeur to a
favored few at the studio and there was a tacit under-
standing that he was to endure the agony of using his
legs to jump out and open the door only for Max Spindell.

He tipped his cap, turned the scar tissue of his face
toward the girl, smiled happily and said, "Evening, Chief.
To the hotel?"

Kiplinger said, "No, Harry, Romanoff's," and Harry's
smile collapsed. Kiplinger added, "We'll go there first."
The smile returned.

The girl was staring silently out of the window, and
finally Kiplinger said, "Does that sound all right to you,
honey? A few martoonies . . . a little chatter . . . early
dinner . . . and then up to my place to get that pretty
little nose of yours down on paper. . . ."

"That sounds fine to me, Mr. Kiplinger. I'd love to,"
he heard her say to the window, but he did not analyze
the tone of her voice too carefully, nor did he look right
at her as she spoke. For he was afraid that she'd turn
toward him and he'd have to look into her eyes, so instead he watched Harry adjusting the rear-view mirror to
go with the sound track. . . .

They sat at a table near the door and ordered drinks,
and everyone who walked past the table looked first at
the girl, then at Kiplinger, then back to the girl, and
many whom Kiplinger knew only casually, and who
usually had nothing to say to him, came over to the table
and said it.

"Is there anyone you *don't* know?" the girl asked. "Is it
always like this?"

"Not always," he said, thinking: It won't be like this

the day after they preview *The Velvet Glove* in Pasadena. It wasn't like this for two whole weeks after *Wherever You Are* was reviewed in the trades. It wasn't like this last night, either. Last night he had dined alone.

One Martini was enough to de-ice her, and during dinner she told him of a young man named Larry who wrote unsuccessful popular music and who had asked her three times to marry him, and she spoke of him just as though she were not fond of him and Kiplinger knew it was because she thought he would like that, and all the time, though he was listening to her, he was thinking only that she was painfully beautiful and ridiculously young and that if she stopped talking for a moment she would probably feel like crying. And it did not make him feel any better to know that he would not blame her.

Sam Winston sat down at their table, swallowed two aspirin tablets, and asked Kiplinger to tell him something funny for the column—but he did not look at Kiplinger as Kiplinger recited a few anecdotes, and when he left he had not taken down a word. A British, second-male-lead came over and was charming and drunk, and a visiting Broadway producer was honest and said simply, "I'm delighted to meet you, Miss Barker," but he let slip a few inappropriate Anglo-Saxonisms in talking with Kiplinger, so the girl excused herself from the table to powder her nose. Then Abner Good, a small, scholarly-looking man, ambled over.

"Rob," he said, "it's nice to see you wallowing in this protoplasmic ooze again. Where you been? Gimme something on *The Velvet Glove*, anything you want. I'll work it into Friday's column."

Kiplinger said, "Abner, I could tell you that it's going to be a sleeper . . . a great psychological thriller with more hitch than Hitchcock. . . . But I won't tell you that because you'll know I'm lying, and besides you printed that last week. So let's not waste time. Get out your pencil."

Abner Good took out a small leather-bound pad and a little gold pencil. He wrote a Hollywood column for a New York racing paper and Broadway columnists appropriated his scoops regularly.

"Her name is Janice Barker," Kiplinger said. "B-a-rk-e-r. Actress, nineteen, will be signed by Spindell to-morrow. I met her this afternoon." He watched Good scribble on the pad.

Good looked up at him. "And?"

"And what?" said Kiplinger, as though he didn't know.

"And?" said Good.

"And I promised her I'd do her portrait for her to-night. After dinner."

Abner Good smiled at his pad. He put it back carefully in his pocket and said, "Thanks, Rob." Kiplinger watched him walk away and he wondered whether Ferdie Saxon would be the first to mail him the clipping.

When the girl returned to the table with fresh makeup and each hair in place, he called the waiter.

"I'm leaving, Paul," he said to the smiling white teeth, "but I was expecting a call here from a Mr. Nick Grandy. Would you please tell the switchboard operator that if anyone by that name calls for me, I'll be at my hotel all evening. She has the number. Remember that—Nick Grandy . . . my hotel."

"You bet, Mr. Kiplinger, I certainly will do that," said the bright teeth. Kiplinger walked out, holding the girl by the arm, and pretended not to see Paul whisper-ing to one of the captains, and he thought what a won-derful joke it would be if Nick Grandy called him at Romanoff's that night, because he did not know a Nick Grandy.

The limousine was waiting for them.

"I got back just in time," Harry explained as they stepped in. "You know them two wise guy actors, the funny fellahs what's always makin' trouble on the lot? Well, tonight, they're so knocked out from playin' touch football all day I hadda lug 'em over to the Turkish baths. But I got back in time, hey, Chief? Leave it to Harry. The hotel, Chief?"

"Right."

"Yeah, I says to myself, Mr. Kiplinger'll be wantin' me in an hour or so, so I hustle them two guys out there in a hurry and beat it back just—"

"I'm glad you did," Kiplinger said. Harry knew practi-cally everyone in the industry and he had a big mouth. "You're a good man, Harry."

"Thanks, Chief," said Harry, adjusting the mirror.

After they had gone several blocks in silence, Kiplinger finally asked the girl, "Happy?"

And she said, "Of course."

He looked out of the window at the far-off lights twinkling up in the hills, for there was no place else to look except at the girl or at the back of Harry's head, which was at alert attention, or at Harry's eyes in the rear-view mirror. So he looked out of the window and wondered whether it was really true that Harry knew more about what went on at the studios than Louella Parsons, and then they were pulling into the driveway, past the wide green lawns, now decolored by the darkness, up to the entrance of the hotel.

"This is it, Chief," said Harry. "Twelve minutes flat, and I coulda done it in ten if that shomiss wasn't giving me the hawk-eye when I was gettin' set to jump the light."

"Nice work, Harry," Kiplinger said, handing him a ten-dollar bill as they got out. "Buy the wife a new mink coat."

"You bet, boss. Much obliged." He grinned once more at the girl, and then he drove off.

They stood on the walk before the hotel until the car was out of sight, and then Kiplinger turned suddenly to the girl and took hold of her hands and he didn't mind now that they were cold.

"Honey," he said, smiling, "thank you, thank you, thank you."

She laughed a little nervously. "I'm afraid I don't quite get it. Thank me for what?"

"Oh . . . let's just say . . . for walking into my office this afternoon, for having dinner with me tonight, for sitting at my table, for riding by my side in Harry's limousine . . . for coming here . . ."

It was too dark to be certain, but he imagined that her eyes were more bewildered than frightened.

He said, "You did enjoy yourself, didn't you?"

And she said, "Well, yes, Mr. Kiplinger, of course."

"And you did want to get into pictures more than anything else in the world, didn't you?"

"Why . . . yes . . . and you don't know how grateful I am, really. I—"

"Oh, but I do, honey," he said. "I certainly do. You told me yourself. You said that you once told Ferdie Saxon you'd do anything to get into pictures."

She looked away, and he said, "You know something? I was that way once myself. I wanted something very badly. That is, there was a somebody I wanted to be. Well, for a while I was young enough and stupid enough to think I was going to get where I wanted, and then I found out it just wasn't going to be. So I made up my mind I'd do anything to get there. And you know what? I got there. Only, I found out something that no one ever told me: getting what you want isn't worth a damn unless the way that you get it is good. And holding onto it is even worse. . . ."

"Don't . . . Please . . ." she blurted out. He wouldn't know if there were tears in her eyes. It was so long since he had seen anything but glycerine. "Mr. Kiplinger, I—"

"No, let me finish," he said. "Tomorrow morning you are going to be given a small job in pictures. It won't be much, but it'll be a beginning. Whether you get any-where, or lose out, will be entirely up to you. You *are* beautiful, but out here that's nothing. If you also have talent, or good luck, you will get where you want. But I want you to promise me something."

"All right," she said, in a very small voice.

"I want you to promise me that if you turn out to be without talent or good luck, you will fail."

She smiled and said, "I promise."

"Good," he said. "And now that I've gotten you a low-paying, nerve-racking job with a talentless studio run by a barbarian named Max Spindell and have exposed you to an evening of brilliant boredom, topped off by my own Grade B speech, I am going to ask you to do me a favor. That is, I want you to keep a deep, dark secret for me. Every girl I've ever asked to keep a secret has managed to do it." He walked her over to a cab parked in the driveway. "Be at Spindell's office at ten sharp. Miss Trueman likes people who are punctual. Get plenty of sleep tonight. Wear your hair loose, the way you're wear-ing it now, and for Pete's sake, smile when you walk in."

"What's this?" she asked, pointing to the cab.

"That's your cab home," he said. He opened the door. "Go on, honey. . . . In."

She got in the back seat and held the door open. "But . . . but I thought there was a secret? And aren't you going to do my portrait? I thought . . ."

"Sure, I'm going to do your picture. I always do."

"But how—?"

"That's the secret, honey, and all I ask is that you please be good to it." He shut the door and looked down at her through the open window. "I'm going to do your portrait from memory," he said. "Just like I've done them all. From memory."

He looked into her eyes and they were smiling now with the rest of her face and she was even more beautiful than he had thought.

"You do believe me, don't you?" he said.

And she said, "Yes, Mr. Kiplinger, I believe you," and somehow he felt that she really did and he was glad that she did, though he knew that it did not matter one way or another.

He said, "One more thing, honey. If your friend Larry asks you a fourth time, why don't you say yes while the music he's writing is still bad? Think about it, will you?"

He started walking away, and she called to him: "It's a deal."

He walked through the lobby to the elevator, and already he was thinking of what brush he would use and what colors he would mix for her hair and how he would capture her eyes as they had been a moment ago. He was no longer tired, and he had an idea this was going to be a good one, perhaps even better than any of the others—and they had been fine jobs, too. And as he went up in the elevator he thought how nice it would be to stay in his apartment for weeks—no, forever—and do nothing but paint, but he knew that that would never be, so he started thinking of the note of appreciation to Ferdie Saxon that he would dictate in the morning, and how Miss Delmar would be able to thrive on it for days, and how he would have nothing to worry about now until *The Velvet Glove* was released, and how even then he would not have to worry because by then there would be another wonderful subject walking in. . . .

Other SIGNET Books You'll Enjoy

THE DEER PARK
Norman Mailer. "One of the most widely discussed books of the season" (*Saturday Review*) exposes with merciless candor the private and public lives of the Hollywood film colony. By the author of *The Naked and The Dead.* (#D1375—50¢)

THE CITY AND THE PILLAR
Gore Vidal. A powerful, highly praised novel of personal tragedy about which the *Atlantic Monthly* said, "A brilliant expose of subterranean life among New York and Hollywood expatriates from normal sex." (#1218—25¢)

EVERYTHING HAPPENS AT NIGHT
(The Late Risers)
Bernard Wolfe. Rowdy and colorful, written by a man who knows his way around Times Square, here is the exciting, inside story of Broadway folk that the *San Francisco Chronicle* called, "an outstanding piece of writing." (#S1238—35¢)

THE MONEY SONG
Arnold Shaw. An absorbing, unusual novel about New York's vivid Tin Pan Alley, a songwriter who dreamed of creating a big-time hit, and his girl who knew all too well the cost of every "money song." (#1145—25¢)

THE CENTER OF THE STAGE
Gerald Sykes. A charming, wilful actress and her scientist-husband fence for dominance in this subtle novel of life in a fashionable Long Island colony. (#1099—25¢)

YOUNG MAN WITH A HORN
Dorothy Baker. The modern classic about the triumphs and tragedy of a young jazz musician who soared to fame but broke his heart striving for an impossible goal. (#1088—25¢)

FRENCH GIRLS ARE VICIOUS
James T. Farrell. Compassionate and dramatic tales of Americans at home and abroad seeking love to fill the void of loneliness. "Stories of biting brilliance . . ." *Philadelphia News.* (#1349—25¢)

NIGHTS OF LOVE AND LAUGHTER
Henry Miller. Devoted exclusively to the work of the dynamic author of *Tropic of Cancer* and other books, this fascinating volume contains many moving tales in a variety of American and European settings. (#S1246—35¢)

THE DELICATE PREY and Other Stories
Paul Bowles. Unusual stories of the violence, passion, and horror that lurks in the hearts of men and women, by an outstanding young American writer, author of *The Sheltering Sky.* (#1296—25¢)

THE UNHOLY THREE and Other Stories
(The Unjustice Collectors)
Louis Auchincloss. In these urbane and striking stories, one of America's most gifted writers, compared by reviewers to Henry James and Edith Wharton, gives a candid picture of frustration and rebellion among the well-to-do. (#1255—25¢)

TO OUR READERS: We welcome your comments about any Signet or Mentor Book, as well as your suggestions for new reprints. If your dealer does not have the books you want, you may order them by mail, enclosing the list price plus 5¢ per copy to cover mailing costs. Send for a copy of our complete catalogue. The New American Library of World Literature, Inc., 501 Madison Ave., New York 22, N. Y.